Rivers turned to Frenchy. "Couple of you boys wedge his right ankle under the outside tire of the trailer and hold him there."

"What are you going to do?" the Iranian's red-haired, freckle-faced companion asked, a lilting brogue in his voice.

Barry looked at him. "I'm going to see how Abdullah here likes life with his ankles crushed."

"This is America," the Irishman said. "Here you have justice and courts and laws and procedures one must follow!"

"No," Barry softly corrected him. "Not here." He pointed to the ground at his feet. "Here you got the Dog!"

Dear Friends,

I've had so many requests for the return of the RIG WAR-
RIOR series that I've finally persuaded my publisher to bring
them back. Here they are—one for each month, in July, August, and September!

Barry Rivers has always been a favorite among the heroes
I've created. Like many an independent thinker, Barry doesn't
like to wait for the slow wheels of justice to turn, so he takes
matters into his own hands. He travels alone—with his trusty
partner, Dog, beside him in his eighteen-wheeler.

I hope you enjoy the RIG WARRIOR books. If you do—or even
if you don't—I'd be happy to hear from you. You can write to
me care of my publisher, or e-mail me at dogcia@aol.com

Happy reading!
Bill Johnstone

RIG WARRIOR

EIGHTEEN-WHEEL AVENGER

William W. Johnstone

PINNACLE BOOKS
Kensington Publishing Corp.
http://www.pinnaclebooks.com

PINNACLE BOOKS are published by

Kensington Publishing Corp.
850 Third Avenue
New York, NY 10022

Copyright © 1988 by William W. Johnstone

All Kensington Titles, Imprints, and Distributed Lines are available at special quantity discounts for bulk purchases for sales promotions, premiums, fund-raising, educational, or institutional use. Special book excerpts or customized printings can also be created to fit specific needs. For details, write or phone the office of the Kensington special sales manager: Kensington Publishing Corp., 850 Third Avenue, New York, NY 10022, attn: Special Sales Department, Phone: 1-800-221-2647

Pinnacle and the P logo Reg. U.S. Pat. & TM Off.

First Printing: August, 1988
First Pinnacle Printing: September, 2000
10 9 8 7 6 5 4 3 2 1

Printed in the United States of America

In baiting a mousetrap with cheese, always leave room for the mouse.

—Saki

1

Barry was bored just about out of his gourd.

He was supposed to be out here not only driving a truck, but also fighting crime and injustice and all those other noble causes . . . doing something besides hauling frozen chicken livers to Denver.

But that was exactly what he was doing. In a truck that carried enough weapons and explosives in hidden compartments to start a major war.

Most of it sitting on top of frozen chicken livers.

After the incident in Kentucky, he had been ordered to cool it. 'Just keep on trucking, Barry. You and Dog. Haul freight,' his contact, Jackson, had told him. 'You'll run into something.'

A four-wheeler came shooting out of an exit ramp, not looking one way or the other.

Barry could do nothing except stand on his brakes and pray to God he didn't jackknife.

He couldn't change lanes. Another four-wheeler had crept up and was staying in his blind spot. But Barry knew the jerk was there.

He got his rig under control and grabbed for his CB mike, spotting a CB antenna on the offending car's trunk.

"You potatohead!" Barry hollered. "Why in hell don't you watch where you're going?"

His Husky, Dog, had been rolled from the bunk and was

now sitting in the seat beside Barry, his lip curled up in a snarl. Dog didn't appreciate being waked up so abruptly.

"Shove it up your butt, driver!" Barry's CB crackled. "You don't own the goddamn road."

"That's right," Barry radioed back. "But I would like to have just a small piece of it to run on."

"I'll give you a big piece of fist you wanna bring that thing over to the shoulder."

"You got it, prick! Name your place."

"Next ramp. Turn to the right. I'll be waiting for you."

"You got it."

Barry knew the other two drivers in their small convoy they'd just put together were listening.

Barry's Cajun temper was boiling over.

"Might be a setup." A voice came through the speaker. "You want some company?"

"I'd appreciate it. I'm called the Dog."

"They call me Ready. Like in ready to go."

"I'm Frenchy." Another voice came in. "You boys can deal me in on this, too. I seen it go down. That four-wheeler's just lookin' for trouble."

Barry saw the car's turn signals flash on. "Then here we go, boys."

"We sure are a long way from nowhere," Ready radioed. "I ain't seen nothing but jackrabbits in an hour."

The drivers slowed and headed down the ramp. Barry cut to the right, the other rigs following. They drove for several miles. Nothing. Barry grabbed his mike.

"I think he was all mouth, boys. We're all alone out here.

"Let's find a place to turn around. Damn, this desert is spooky at night."

The big rigs moved slowly up the road, Barry leading the way, looking for a place to turn around. He was getting a hard knot of suspicion in the pit of his stomach. He tried to remember just where that car had come from. It seemed to have appeared out of nowhere.

And the four-wheeler who'd been crowding him on Barry's blind side—where had it gone?

The more he thought about it, the more he didn't like it.

It smelled of setup.

But why would anybody go to all that trouble to hijack a load of chicken livers?

Barry grabbed his mike and said, "Don't roll down your windows, boys. Lock your doors. I got a bad feeling about this."

"I hear that," Frenchy radioed back. "What you haulin', Dog?"

"Frozen chicken livers. You?"

"Disposable diapers. Ready?"

"Tools." He laughed. "I reckon somebody could use the tools to break open the boxes of chicken livers and the diapers for napkins. That pretty well lets out any thought of hijack, don't it."

"Unless they got us mixed up with somebody else," Barry radioed.

"And bear in mind whoever set us up is listenin' to every damn word we're sayin'," Frenchy reminded them.

"Buildings up ahead," Barry told his unknown friends. "Probably be a place to turn around."

The old road had deteriorated to the point of being nonexistent. The buildings had been long-abandoned; what remained were crumbling ruins, silent reminders of something that had failed.

"See them tire tracks off to the west?" Frenchy asked. "A lot of them. I don't like this, boys."

"Trucks left those tracks," Ready said. "A lot of trucks. I think, boys, we got ourselves into something that we don't want to be in."

Barry glanced in his mirrors. He cursed. "Lights coming up fast behind us."

"We try to turn around in that sand and we're gonna be here for the duration," Ready hollered.

"You boys are about to see something," Barry radioed. "And for your sake, you better forget you ever saw it."

Barry reached behind him, into a cargo bag, and lifted out an Uzi SMG.

The three-rig convoy had stopped on the broken and rutted old road.

"What are you talkin' about, Dog?" Frenchy called.

Barry jacked a round into the Uzi and stuck several full clips behind his belt just as the two pickup trucks behind them came to a sliding stop, men pouring out of the cabs.

The men were all armed with shotguns and pistols.

"Get out of them trucks and keep your hands in sight!" a man yelled. He held in his hands what looked to Barry to be a 9mm pistol.

Barry lowered his window and gave the man a short burst from the Uzi. The 9mm slugs knocked the man spinning around in the New Mexico sand. When his macabre death-dance had concluded, he fell sprawling to the sand.

Still sitting in the cab of his Kenworth, Barry steadied the Uzi and emptied the clip into the line of armed men, knocking most of them sprawling. While he was sliding in a fresh clip, two men ran to a pickup truck and spun away, heading up the broken old road, away from the Interstate.

Barry climbed down from his cab and cautiously walked over to the staggered row of dead and dying and seriously hurt would-be hijackers.

Ready and Frenchy climbed down, both of them wearing shocked looks, and joined Barry.

"Holy bejesus, Dog!" Ready blurted. "You play for keeps, don't you?"

"Better them than us, wouldn't you say?" He looked at the man under the full hunter's moon that illuminated the desert.

"The man does have a point," Frenchy summed it up.

"Tell y'all what," Ready drawled. "We better start making plans to haul out of here. 'Fore the cops come."

"There won't be any cops," Barry told him, kneeling down

beside one of the men who was still breathing. "Not until daylight and this scene is spotted from the air."

He rolled the man over onto his back. His stomach and chest were bloody from the 9mm slugs. He didn't have a whole lot of time left him.

"You bastard!" the dying man spat at Barry. "The boss said you was with us. You goddamn traitors!"

"The boss?"

"Fuck you!"

"Funny name for a man," Ready said. "How come y'all wanted chicken livers and diapers and tools?"

"What?" the grounded man gasped.

"You heard him," Frenchy urged. "Are you guys crazy or something?"

"Either that, or they got a lot of kids and old cars to work on," Ready suggested.

"You're all dead meat," the dying man told him. "We'll get you. Somebody will. You goddamn SST haulers have made your last run."

The highjacker was just seconds away from taking his last run.

"I ain't never pulled no safe secure transport," Frenchy said. He looked at Ready. "You?"

"Long time ago. But that was some years back."

"All SST drivers are armed," Barry said. "And usually run with armed escorts."

The dying man spoke his last words. "All three of you are independents. We got your names and numbers. You're dead meat."

He closed his eyes and double-clutched his way across the dark river.

"Let's find a common denominator," Barry suggested, pulling out the dead man's wallet. He checked the driver's license. "O'Brian."

Frenchy, with a grimace on his face, removed the wallet of another. "Kelly's this guy's last name."

Ready said, "Kildare."

The last driver's license was in the name of Fitzgerald.

"All right." Frenchy stood up, looking at Barry. "So what the hell does this prove?"

"Irish." Barry pocketed the driver's licenses. "They're all Irish names."

"I don't make the connection," Ready admitted.

"Maybe there isn't one," Barry thought aloud. "But I'd make a bet there is."

"And that is. . . ?" Frenchy asked.

"They got us confused with a three-truck SST convoy. One that was going to cooperate and hand over their cargoes. Weapons, more than likely."

"Weapons!" Ready looked puzzled. "I don't get it, Dog."

"For the IRA."

"Ahhh!" Ready got it then. "Those terrorists over in Ireland who're always blowing things up and killin' civilians?"

"To many people in Ireland, Ready, they're not terrorists. They're heroes. Fighting for a free Ireland." He looked at his new friends. "Get yourselves armed. Plenty of weapons on the ground. Get a pistol and a shotgun. Take whatever ammo you can find. Go on, do it."

Reluctantly, Ready and Frenchy obeyed, picking through the gore of the recently departed.

They faced Barry, Frenchy asking, "Now what?"

"Where are you boys heading?"

All three of them were heading for Denver.

"You heard the man." Barry pointed to the hijacker who'd warned them they were dead meat. "We stick close together 'cause there's gonna be people looking for us. We drop off our loads in Denver, we'll sit down and talk this thing out."

"We just leave the bodies?" Frenchy asked.

"What do you want to do with them?"

"Well, ah, hell! I don't know."

Ready looked at Barry in the moonlight. "Man, you're a real hard-ass, you know that?"

"So I've been told." He looked at the men, one at a time. He judged them both to be around his age. "You boys veterans?"

They were. Both of them Army. Served in 'Nam. Grunts.

"Then you're not cherries when it comes to firearms or seeing dead bodies or pulling a trigger?"

"That was a long time ago, Dog," Frenchy said.

"What are you gettin' at, Dog?" Ready asked.

"We're in trouble, boys, if I'm correctly reading what happened tonight. Obviously, those guys who got away have our truck plates, some permit numbers, home base; enough to track us down. And the IRA doesn't screw around, boys. Some of their own are dead. And they'll be looking for revenge."

Neither man spoke as his words sank in.

"If you want to cut out and try it on your own," Barry suggested, "I certainly won't blame you."

"The damn rumors are true." Ready was the first to speak.

"What rumors?" Frenchy asked.

"The rumors that many drivers don't talk about on the air. About that driver with some kind of government protection, or something like that. Runnin' around like a modern-day Robin Hood. It just come to me. That guy's handle is supposed to be Dog."

"I thought all that was just a bunch of crap somebody made up."

"How many truckers you know carry a machine gun around with them? And God only knows what else."

Both drivers turned to face Barry.

"How about it, boys?"

"Let's get the hell out of here, Dog!" Frenchy said. "We're right behind you."

They rolled on through the night, crossing into Colorado just at dawn. They pulled over at a truck stop and parked close. After breakfast, they crawled into their sleepers for a few hours' rest.

Barry was the first one up. He walked Dog and put him back into the truck, then went into the truck stop and put in a call to his Washington contact, Jackson.

"You're still hot, Dog," Jackson told him. "So just keep on trucking."

"Shut up and listen," Barry said.

He brought the man up to date.

Jackson was silent for a few heartbeats. Barry could hear his sigh over the phone. "Okay. I'll get with the Department of Energy and tell them what you've told me. Frenchy and Ready. What are their last names?"

"Hell, I don't know. I never asked."

"Well, ask! You're all three about to become SST men."

"Maybe they don't want to do that."

"Use your persuasive charm, Dog. And think of three other drivers while you're at it. And call me from Denver."

The line went dead.

"I thought all the SSTs hauled was nuclear stuff," Ready said. "Was when I did a bit of it."

"They've changed some," Barry told him. "My Kenworth is armored with bulletproof glass. Steel-plated bottom."

"I know that's one hell of a nice rig you got," Frenchy told him.

Barry's Kenworth was all of that, and more. It was his home. His only home.

He shook away the memories. But they would be back. They always came back.

"You got a funny look on your face, Dog. What is your whole name, anyway?"

"Barry Rivera."

The Dog.

2

His name had been Barry Rivers. He had once been a very successful arms dealer and consultant, known worldwide.

All that changed when a bomb meant to kill him instead killed his new wife, Kate. Little Kate. Blue-eyed Kate, with the corn-yellow hair.

Barry spent months in a military hospital. There, the doctors reworked his face, reshaped his eyes, his nose. He spent more weeks rebuilding his hospital-atrophied muscles.

He met with several government men, usually Jackson or Weston. He liked their plan, but he wanted to hear it from The Man himself.

Then one day the President walked into Barry's hospital room.

"You're a stubborn man, Mr. Rivera."

"I'm still Rivers until we can reach an agreement, Mr. President."

The President smiled. "The only SST rig on the road with only one driver. Dog and Dog. That's not a very friendly dog, either. He bites."

"So do I."

"I hope so."

"I pick my targets."

"Most of the time. Agreed."

"Fine. Whatever I ask for, in the way of weapons or explosives—I get. Immediately."

"Agreed."

The Dog and the President talked for more than an hour, firming things up.

The President shook Barry's hand. "Glad to have you with us, Barry."

"Call me Dog."

"Smooth and Mustard is lookin' for work," Frenchy suggested. "They can drive anything with wheels on it and they're both 'Nam vets."

"Fine. Get in touch with them. Right now. I prefer to go it alone, anyway."

"Well," Ready said, standing up and stretching. "It's steady work."

"It's also a good way to get killed," Barry reminded them both.

"What's that they say about safety in numbers?" Frenchy smiled.

"Get some sleep," Barry told them. "I got a hunch we'll be pulling out early in the morning."

The phone woke him up at four in the morning. Jackson.

"Don't you ever sleep, Jackson?"

"Your other drivers are on their way to Kirtland Air Force Base in Albuquerque. And I picked up a codriver for you. Meet you there. A Lieutenant Cutter, with the Air Force's U.S. SOCOM."

"What the hell is that?"

"Special Operations Command. They're tough and the best in the business in dealing with terrorists. Cutter will be your codriver. Don't argue. You need one and you know it."

"Fine. What's the procedure for Frenchy and Ready to get to Kirtland?"

"Plane. Get them out to Stapleton by eight o'clock. I know

how you are about that truck of yours. Just get down there in twenty-four hours. They'll use that time to familiarize themselves with the regular SST tractors. Orders will be forthcoming. See you."

The connection was broken.

Frenchy and Barry had to get Ready drunk before he'd even discuss getting on a plane.

"I hate planes. I don't trust planes. I don't like planes. And I ain't gettin' on no damn airplane!"

Finally Barry put in a call to Jackson. Jackson was out, but Weston was in. Barry explained the situation.

When Weston was through cussing, he said, "Hang on. I'll get an Air Force plane. Get him drunk as a skunk and pour him in the plane."

Barry waved bye-bye and got a taxi back to his motel. He paid up, checked out, and hit the road. It was about four hundred and fifty miles to Kirtland.

He looked over at Dog, sitting in the seat. "You ready, boy?"

Dog growled.

Dog and Dog hit the road.

It wasn't long before Barry realized he'd picked up a tail. And his followers weren't trying to be secretive about it. They were on his donkey and wanted him to know it.

He was running empty, and the big Kenworth could practically fly if Barry wanted to pedal the metal; but with a smile on his face, he decided to see just what his followers had in mind.

Long before he got to Colorado Springs, Barry had picked up his pace car, and like the car following him, the car in front had three men in it.

From the quick looks he'd gotten, none of the six looked real friendly. Barry decided he'd wait for a particularly desolate stretch of road, between Pueblo and Walsenburg, before making any moves. He wished his followers would open the dance. Then he could slap one off the road with a clear conscience.

As it now stood, he was ten percent unsure the two cars held people who had unkind thoughts toward him. And unlike terrorists, he did not wish to be responsible for the deaths of innocents.

Coming out of Pueblo, rolling south, Barry listened to his CB. No Bears in sight and none had been spotted on the fifty-mile stretch between Pueblo and Walsenburg.

Barry decided to make his move.

He swung over in the left lane and let the big Kenworth howl; the 350 NTC Cummins kicked in hard and Barry blew past the Ford car. Barry caught a quick glimpse of three startled faces.

He also caught a glimpse of what looked to be an M-16 on the rear seat; the lone passenger in the back with a hand on the weapon.

Barry stayed in the left lane and switched on his scanner. The red light danced left and right and back and forth before finally settling on channel 2.

"What the hell's he doing?" came the excited voice.

"Don't know. But I think he's made us."

"What next?"

"Do we take him out?" a third voice came in.

"Yes. No more talk. Take him."

The red light again began its frantic racing. Barry clicked off the scanner and got ready.

He didn't have a long wait. He checked his mirrors. The two dark sedans were all that he could see behind him. Nothing in front of him.

"Come on, assholes!" Barry muttered. "Let's do it."

This was the very reason SSTs always carried a three-person crew. Always a codriver and a person in the sleeper. All heavily armed. And usually with a four-wheeler pacing or in the drag. Whether an SST is carrying 2 kilograms of plutonium or the business end of a Minuteman missile, the threat of sabotage or hijack is always there. With terrorism full-blown in America, the possibilities of an SST getting struck were growing daily.

The lead sedan began closing as Barry stayed in the left lane. He could see the rear window, left side, lower. The M-16 was in plain view now.

Now the intentions of his pursuers were known.

Barry peeled back his lips in a snarl.

Dog cut his eyes toward Barry and joined him in the snarling.

"Bed, Dog!" Barry yelled over the high howling of the Cummins.

Dog jumped from the seat to the custom bunk and lay down, out of harm's way.

The sedan was just about right to take out. Just a few more yards.

Barry slowed a couple of mph and smiled as the driver in the car took the bait.

Barry could see the grim faces of the men in the front seat of the car. The man on the passenger side was armed with what appeared to be a shotgun.

The car in the drag had stayed back.

As the sedan pulled even with Barry's trailer, he swung the trailer slightly. Traveling at 70 mph, the trailer smacked the car. The driver of the car fought the wheel as his right-side tires left the interstate and hit the shoulder.

Once more under control, but with its left side dented from the impact, the sedan made a move.

Barry simply cut the wheel slightly and ran the car off the road. It crashed through the guardrail and went sailing off, carrying its three terrorists into a very dubious meeting with eternity.

The second car braked to a smoking stop and pulled off onto the shoulder. Barry, with a smile on his face, kept on trucking. He patted the seat beside him and Dog was instantly there.

"Three less baby killers in the world, Dog."

Dog barked.

"But their buddies will be coming after us, you can bet on that."

Dog snarled.

"Yeah. That's the way I feel about it, Dog. Let the bastards come on!"

Security at the gate checked his ID and waved him on through, but not before the security police gave him some sidewise looks.

Obviously they had been told to ask no questions.

Barry made his way slowly toward the area he'd been pointed by security, stopped, and shut it down.

He was walking Dog when Jackson came out of a building and walked toward him.

"Keep that damn dog on the leash, Barry. He bites."

"No worse than the guy holding the other end of the leash, Jackson."

Jackson grimaced.

"You have any trouble on the way down?"

Barry smiled.

Jackson sighed. "Just think, I gave up a nice secure, reasonably peaceful job to look after you. What happened, Barry?"

Barry explained about the incident on the interstate.

"You check to see if they were dead?"

"Nope. But the car sailed about a hundred feet, then rolled end over end. If they're not dead, they're not going to be doing much terrorizing for a long time."

"I'll check with the CHP about it. Let's go somewhere and talk. I think, unknowingly, you've dropped right into the middle of one hell of a big operation. Heads up, Barry. These guys play rough."

"No kidding," Barry said sarcastically.

Barry made sure Dog had done his business and then put him back in the Kenworth, with food and fresh water. Dog promptly flopped down and went to sleep.

Barry walked across the compound to the concrete block building where Jackson had told him he'd be waiting . . . with some people he wanted Barry to meet.

One person in particular caught and held Barry's attention. A dark-eyed, dark-haired, tanned, and extremely fit appearing lady. Barry could tell that when she stood up, she was going to very nearly be able to flat-footed look him in the eyes. Barry was five-ten; he guessed the lady to be close to five-nine. She was magnificent-looking, her eyes shining with that glow of a person in the best of physical condition.

Jackson said, "Barry, these people are part of an Air Force special team. They've been bounced around so much over the past few years, they're probably beginning to feel like homeless children. Right now, they come under the Air Force's SOCOM. They're the best in the business when dealing with terrorism."

Captain Barnett. Lieutenant Jamison. Sergeant Halleck. Sergeant Gale. And Lieutenant Cutter—the fine-looking woman.

It dawned on Barry: Lieutenant *Cutter!*

He turned to Jackson. "Are you telling me that she. . . ?" He pointed to the woman.

"That is correct, Barry." Jackson's reply was smooth. "Her father owned a very successful trucking firm in the midwest. She grew up behind the wheel of a truck. She'll be your co-driver. Barry Rivera, meet Meri Cutter."

The woman stood up. Great God! Barry thought, eyeballing her from her bloused jump boots to the top of her short dark hair. What a woman.

He nodded at her.

She nodded at him, her eyes cool as she appraised him.

"You like dogs, Cutter?"

"I love dogs. Why?"

"Because I travel with one. A Husky."

"What's his name? Assuming it is a he."

"It's a he. Dog."

She allowed herself a small smile. "And I believe from what

Jackson has told us—which isn't much—that you are code-named Dog."

"That is correct."

"Quite a combination. Dog and Dog."

Captain Barnett stood up and shook hands with Barry. "Jackson has told us very little about you, Barry. And none of us will push for further information concerning your present operation or how you came to be. But since this operation was put together very quickly, we haven't had time to read your dossier. . . ."

"He doesn't have one," Jackson said quickly.

The personnel of the SOCOM shifted uncomfortably and cut their eyes to Jackson. "What do you mean, sir?" Sergeant Gale asked.

"Just what I said, Sergeant. Suffice it to say that Barry was a captain of a special forces A-team. He helped set up and train that, ah, group of people that presidents are hesitant to use against terrorists because of several weak-kneed members of Congress."

The AF team smiled at that.

Jackson continued, "Barry is highly trained and very competent. But he prefers to work alone."

"Doing what?" Barnett asked.

"And for whom?" Cutter added.

Jackson's eyes were bleak. "You do not have a need to know."

"Going to be an interesting operation," Lieutenant Jamison muttered.

"More so than you might think." Jackson looked at him. "The Dog has carte blanche in his dealings."

The AF team became immediately much more interested and much more attentive.

"Are you saying that we can use whatever tactics we deem suitable or advisable in dealing with these terrorists?" Barnett asked.

"That is correct. The Dog operates under his own rules. He is answerable to only one person."

None of the AF team asked who that one person was. That

was none of their business and all knew Jackson wouldn't tell them anyway.

Cutter's eyes remained fixed on Barry. About forty, she guessed. Hard-looking. Just a touch of gray at the temples. Deep blue eyes. Almost black. Rugged-looking. Handsome, but not in that sissy pretty-boy way that Meri abhorred.

She wondered who that one person was that Barry answered to.

But she was too well-trained to consider asking.

"Let's get down to it," Jackson said, putting an end to Meri's appraisal of Barry. For the moment.

After a hard hour of questions and answers and trying to fit together the pieces of the puzzle, the team was not much closer to getting an accurate assessment of just who they were up against.

Jackson called for a break.

"Come on," Barry said to Cutter. "You'd better meet Dog and get yourself acquainted with my rig."

"Have you met the other guys?" Barry asked, as they walked across the compound to his truck.

Meri allowed herself a smile. "Yes. Like most drivers they're all full of crap, but they'll stand, I believe. We've run a good check on them, considering the minimal amount of time we had to do it in, and they all checked out clean. They all have good service records."

"I'm ashamed to say that I don't even know if any of them are married."

"All of them are married. Are you?"

"Not anymore."

"Divorced?"

"Once. My second wife was killed."

"I'm sorry."

"So am I."

She dropped the subject.

Meri met Dog and the two of them hit it off from the outset. She sat down behind the wheel of Barry's custom Kenworth and smiled.

"I feel like I'm back home," she said.

A Kenworth conventional with a lot of modification and custom work. Smoked windows. The best sound system available. Twin airhorns and twin spots, remote controlled. A built-in bank of radios, CB and police band, whose crystals could be easily changed. Steer Safe stabilizers. Quartz halogen driving lights. The front of the tractor was beefed up with heavy steel mesh, protecting lights and grill in case Barry was forced to ram. Which he had done several times. Airglide 100 suspension. All glass was bulletproof. The cab had reinforced armor plate all around, insulated and fireproof. If they were ever ambushed, a button could be pushed that would lock the axles so that only a cutting torch could free them, unless the driver reset the button.

Alcoa aluminum ten-hole Budd wheels. Fuller Roadranger thirteen-speed transmission. The differentials were 3.73 Rockwells SQHP. Fontaine fifth wheel. Michelin steelbelt tires, 1100x24.5 tubeless. Air dryer for air brake. Jake brake. The sleeper was full customized. Walk-in. Electrowarmth mattress with mirrors and a twelve-volt TV.

"What are we going to be hauling, if anything?" she asked.

"I don't know. But I would imagine, since none of the others in your team drive eighteen-wheelers, they'll be pacing us in four-wheelers. That's just a guess."

"I doubt it. They'll be out in the field, more than likely. Working on information we feed them. And that's just a guess."

Barry nodded. Something about this woman caught and held his attention. He did not think there was much, if any, sexual harassment within her team. Meri looked like she could handle any situation that might confront her. Her hands were carefully kept feminine-looking, but the calluses on the inside of her palms were real. Barry suspected she was an expert in several forms of martial arts.

"This is a unique operation you have going, Barry. Dealing

out justice from the cab of an eighteen-wheeler. If that's what you do," she quickly added.

"Yeah." He smiled at her. "It's sort of like an elephant trying to tiptoe through a china shop."

3

Ready and Frenchy introduced Barry to Smooth and Mustard.

"I like mustard greens," the man said with a grin.

"I ain't tellin' nobody how my handle got hung on me," Smooth announced. "Ain't done it before, don't intend to start now."

All the drivers in Barry's new team—with the exception of Cutter—were about forty, give or take a year or two, with many, many years of experience behind the wheel of an eighteen-wheeler. Their dossiers that the AF team had complied on them showed no drug use. They all enjoyed their beer, but not on the job. They all had wives, kids, mortgages, hopes, dreams.

Good, solid, steady men. Blue jeans and cowboy boots and country music.

"Let's get you checked out with weapons," Cutter said.

"Yes, *ma'am!*" Mustard said.

It didn't take long for all of them to bring back to the fore their expertise with the M-16. The newer model, which when set on auto, fired in short bursts. They were checked out with pistols: the Beretta 9mm. The men were all adequate-to-good pistol shots. They were given sawed-off pump shotguns. 12 gauge. Loaded with double-ought buckshot.

The remainder of the AF special operations team appeared at the range, all of them dressed in civilian clothing.

"We're heading up to Colorado," Barnett told Cutter and Barry. "To the scene of your, ah, accident, Barry. You and your people will be here for a couple more days, and then orders will be cut and you'll pick up a shipment of weapons. It's going to be a deliberate long run for you. All the way across country. You and your people will be the bait."

"I understand."

"Hang in, Cutter."

When the AF special team had left, Barry turned to look at Cutter, who was certainly pleasing to the eyes. "Get changed into civilian clothes, Meri; out of those field clothes. We're going to take a run in my rig. I want to see how you operate."

She operated very well, Barry thought, after deliberately putting her in a couple of tight situations—right in the middle of downtown Albuquerque. They headed south on Interstate 25, cut east on highway 60, back north on 285, and then back to the base on Interstate 40.

He put her through the paces and she handled herself well. Rusty at first, for it had been several years since she'd sat behind the wheel of an 18-wheeler, but as the miles rolled by, her confidence returned. Barry made no effort to hide his smile as they pulled into the compound at Kirtland and Cutter deliberately backed between the rigs of Ready and Frenchy—with just about two inches to spare on either side of the mirrors.

Meri shut the rig down and looked at Barry. "Did I pass, teacher?"

"With flying colors, Cutter. Now the hard part begins."

"And that is?"

"We start getting shot at."

* * *

It came as no surprise to Barry when Jackson informed them they would be confined to the base for the duration. Barry had already warned his drivers to expect that.

And he also warned them that they had best get some rest, for he had a hunch that tomorrow they would start undergoing some hard-assed training.

They were shown the building where they would live during their time at Kirtland; it was comfortable, with a pool table, TVs, and separate living quarters. Their meals would be brought to them.

"I feel like I'm back in the goddamn Army!" Mustard bitched.

"You are," Barry told him. "In a manner of speaking. And," he warned them, "this is going to be just as dangerous and deadly as 'Nam. So pay attention to what your instructors tell you. They're trying not only to teach you all something about terrorists and how they act, but also to possibly save your lives. I'll see you all in the morning."

He left them with that. He had subdued them considerably.

Barry stepped outside just as dusk was gently pushing aside the day. Cutter was sitting on the steps in front of the building.

Barry sat down beside her.

Without looking at him, she said, "All our intelligence is showing the various terrorist groups around the world are linking up. Some more than others, of course. But it is coming together."

"Bottom line?"

"America is going to get a hard jolt back into reality, very soon, we believe. If it isn't too late for us."

"You believe it is?"

"Borderlining."

"Well, at last something is coming along that I can sink my teeth into."

She met his eyes. Ten thousand questions in them. Questions he knew she would never ask.

"We'll be operating from both sides of the law, Barry. I'm

not telling you anything you don't already know. But I feel it's something the other drivers should know."

"You know as well as I do that ninety-nine percent of this country's truck drivers are red, white and blue Americans. Whatever it takes to combat terrorism, they'll do, and to hell with the do-gooders who moan about the rights of criminals."

Her smile was hard. "Without asking any leading questions about just what exactly you do . . . How many truckers do you believe are aware of you?"

"Quite a few. But I'm not discussed on the CBs."

She nodded her head. Barry knew there would be no more questions about his life.

His life. His past life. Kate.

They had not been married long. Heading back to his offices outside Washington. Barry, Kate, Dog. Traveling in Barry's pickup with the camper top.

They had enjoyed a late breakfast and then packed up. Kate got behind the wheel.

Dog barked.

"Maybe he wants to go for a walk," Kate said, smiling at him, blue eyes shining. "You take him. I'll warm up the truck."

"Come on, Dog," Barry said. "Time for you to do your business."

Barry and Dog walked across the concrete to the grassy area. While Dog ran and sniffed, looking for a good spot to mark, Barry heard the pickup's engine crack. White-hot heat struck him hard, just as a tremendous sound wave knocked him sprawling to the ground. Out of his blurring and shocked eyes, he could see Dog rolling end over end on the ground. He could hear the sounds of falling debris: chunks of metal and glass and plastic hitting the earth.

Barry could feel a warm stickiness running down his face. Blood.

He was burning; his shirt was on fire.

But where was the pain?

He tried to roll over. He could not. None of his extremities would obey commands from his brain. Red tinged with a strange darkness began enveloping him as the pain reached him.

Dog was barking, an angry note to the sound.

"Kate!" Barry yelled, but her name was only a whisper coming out of his mouth.

And then Barry knew nothing as a cold hand touched him lightly with bony fingers.

"You went away," Cutter said.

"I do that every now and then. But never on the job," Barry assured her.

"I'd like to talk more, but I'm afraid of stepping over into sensitive areas."

"I'll let you know if that happens."

"How'd you get into the business you're in?"

"You just stepped over. How did you get into this business?"

"He said, shifting smoothly." She laughed. "ROTC in college. Before I even got through my second year, they discovered I had a flair for the clandestine. They made me an offer I couldn't refuse, so to speak. OCS. A lot of school. Worked for a time with the AF Office of Special Investigations. That was mostly analysis of field intelligence and weaponry training. Went through some CIA training and learned to blow things up and also to think and act like terrorists. That's very important when dealing with those kinds of nitwits. I've been overseas, working with foreign governments in tracking down threats to U.S. facilities and aiding in the interrogations."

"Your life has been interesting, to say the least."

"Somehow," she said drily, "I have this feeling my life has not been nearly as interesting as yours."

"Don't give up hoping."

"Well, the sad thing about all this terrorism business, is that while we can train personnel from CIA, DOE, ATF, State Department and the various services—and we do—we are forbidden to teach civilian police. And that's sad. Because it's the local cops who are going to have to bear the brunt of dealing with terrorism when it hits our shores. And it's coming. Very soon."

Ready and Frenchy and Smooth and Mustard had stepped out of the building, standing behind Barry and Cutter, quietly listening.

"You boys join us," Barry motioned for them to gather around on the steps. "We're going back to school." When they had made themselves as comfortable as possible, Barry asked Cutter, "Bring us up to date, please."

"That would take weeks. I'll give you a thumbnail report. Let's start with the IRA. The Irish Republican Army. Some of them are freedom fighters, but not this bunch. They're extremists—a splinter group known as I-7 just as bad as any terrorist group working anywhere around the globe. They torture, they rape, they maim, they kill, they destroy. They're terrorists, any way one wants to look at it logically.

"The Irish-Americans don't want to be told and don't believe it when we try to tell them that certain elements within the IRA—breakaway groups such as I-7—have direct links with the Palestinian terrorists, the E.T.A.—that's the Basque Separatist Movement—the Bader-Meinhof gang and the Red Brigades. And that's just naming a few.

"It may be difficult for you men to believe, but we know that for the past two decades, terrorist groups have been cooperating closely, even when they have no philosophical or political grounds to share. They train together. They oftentimes share the same instructors. They provide safe houses for each other. They also collaborate in the buying and the smuggling of weapons. Damn it!" She spat out the word. "When someone helps one terrorist group they're helping them all."

The door had opened and closed.

"How are they working the money end of it?" Barry asked.

"What do you mean?" She looked up as Smooth handed her a can of beer. "Thanks."

He passed the beer around. Compliments of the United States Air Force.

"More specifically, the buying of arms."

"Well, say a bank or an armored car is knocked over in . . . well, wherever . . . London. That money is very unlikely to be used to buy guns for the I-7 directly. For obvious reasons."

She waited for Barry to pick it up. He did.

"The connection would be too easy to trace."

"Right. So instead, a dummy company will have been set up in, say, Italy or Greece or Switzerland and that money will be used to buy guns and bombs for the ETA. Then the Spanish Separatists may well use monies collected for the IRA in America to buy guns from Lebanon. A combined smuggling operation is then set up—part to go to the Basque, part to go to the I-7."

"Slick," Mustard muttered. "These guys we're dealing with ain't idiots."

"Far from it. Many are highly educated. At some of the finest schools in the world. Some are just streetwise, educated by the best terrorist trainers to be found."

"I'm curious about something," Barry said, after a swig of beer. "Why doesn't the Department of Justice move in on groups like this NORAID and put them out of business?"

"They tried. They're still trying. Under the terms of the Foreign Agents Registration Act, NORAID has had an office in Belfast since the early 1970s. Many NORAID associates have been arrested and convicted; but still the group claims they are a charity working to provide aid for the victims of British terrorism in Northern Ireland. And of course, any thinking person knows that is nothing more than pure bullshit."

"How many Americans contribute to the I-7?" Frenchy asked.

"We don't know, although it's believed that some Americans do make substantial contributions, and they know perfectly well their money is going to kill people. But they have been brainwashed into believing their money is going to a fine and noble cause. Fighting for freedom."

"Well, I'm dumb," Smooth said, "but I ain't *that* dumb!"

"Neither are those who contribute," Cutter replied, disgust thickening her voice. "That's what I mean about the contributors knowing they are buying guns and bombs to kill people."

"I wonder how high up in our government this thing goes?" Barry asked, the question not directed at anyone in particular.

"Meaning. . . ?" Cutter looked at him.

He met her gaze. "Elected, appointed, or civil service employees."

She shrugged. "We have reason to believe that some in our government may support I-7 but no proof that they ever directly gave aid to I-7 or any other terrorist group."

They sat for a time in the New Mexico night, Cutter sipping at her beer, Barry and the others silently absorbing all that she had told them.

Ready said, "I seen a lot of old people and babies killed in 'Nam. Well, not a lot, but a hell of a lot more than I wanted to see. I don't believe in terrorism. No matter what the cause. It's just wrong." He stood up and walked into the building, the other drivers following him one by one.

Cutter stood up. "Going to be a long day tomorrow, Barry. Good night."

Barry sat for a time, holding his empty can. He felt the past slipping up on him, as it sometimes did when a particular mood struck him, touching him with gentle hands of remembrance.

He had taken a leave of absence from his Maryland firm; Barry hadn't had a vacation in years. He had tossed some gear into his pickup truck and headed south, to New Orleans, to see his father, Big Joe Rivers, who ran a large trucking company. His CB had conked out on him just outside of Biloxi, on Interstate 10, and he had pulled into a truck stop. After a sandwich, he bought a new Midland and installed it.

"You gonna test that thing out, Citizen?" a female voice spoke from behind him.

Barry turned, and looked into the face of an angel.

"Uh . . . yeah. Just as soon as I get on the road."

"Which way you headin'?"

She was perhaps five-three. Blonde. Hair the color of corn. A traffic-stopping figure. Blue eyes.

"West. Into New Orleans."

"Yeah? Me, too. You watch them motherfuckin' cops just this side of Slidell. They'll nail your ass to the wall."

An angel with a garbage can for a mouth.

Barry stared at her.

"You ever drive a truck, boy?"

"Long time ago. Why, does it show?"

"Yeah. Kind of, I guess. You lookin' for a job?"

"Could be. Who do you drive for?"

"Big Joe Rivers."

Barry had to hide his smile. He'd make a bet this little waif-looking blonde watched her gutter mouth around his dad. Big Joe could and did cuss . . . but not around women, and he didn't like women using bad language.

"Yeah? I've heard talk about Rivers Trucking. About them having mob troubles. Maybe I'd prefer to eat less and go on living."

She put both hands on shapely hips and hung a cussin' on Barry. "Goddamnchickenshityankeebastard!"

Barry laughed at this mighty mite. "Whoa! I didn't say I wasn't interested. I'm just telling you what I heard, that's all."

"This dude givin' you trouble, Kate?" a man's voice came from behind Barry.

Barry cut his eyes. A driver holding a wooden tire knocker stood just behind them.

"Goddamn coward is all!" She spat the words.

"Maybe he's just got good sense," another voice was added.

Kate whirled around. "What the hell do you mean, Cottonmouth?"

"I heard it all. Just gettin' out of my bunk. This guy didn't do nothin' to deserve that cussin' you hung on him. You can't blame a man for wantin' to stay alive."

"Why don't you take that boot you're holdin' and stuff it in your mouth?" Kate yelled at him. "And stay the hell out of my business."

"Whoa!" Barry said, holding up a hand. Cottonmouth was hopping around, trying unsuccessfully to tug on his boot. "This thing is getting out of hand."

"Well, you just apologize to Kate and we'll forget it," the East Texas Motor Freight man said.

Barry looked at him. "Apologize? For what?"

" 'Cause I said so, buddy,"

Barry's Cajun temper was rapidly coming to the boiling point. "Partner," he said to the ETMF driver, "you better get off my back before I kick your butt so hard you're gonna feel like you been ridin' that camel all day instead of your rig." He pointed to the logo painted on the trailer of the ETMF man.

"He probably feels that way now," a third man spoke. "I drove something that raggedly-assed lookin', I'd be ashamed to call myself a trucker."

Truck drivers insult each other on the average of about ten thousand times a day—per state. The ETMF man just grinned. But his grin was not directed toward Barry.

"You gonna apologize, boy?"

"Hell, no!" Barry told him.

"Then I think I'll just whip your ass."

"With or without your club, hotshot?"

The tire knocker was tossed to the man who'd insulted him. "Hold that. And don't steal it, you hound-dog-lookin' thing."

"Hell, who'd want it!"

The driver grinned at Barry and swung. But Barry had anticipated the punch and sidestepped it. The ETMF man slipped on a grease spot and fell down.

"Them are brand-new jeans!" he bitched.

"Damn, boy!" Kate yelled. "Defendin' me is one thing, but you gotta stand up to do it!"

"Give me time, Kate!"

"I ought to kick your face in," Barry told the man. "But I feel sorry for you. If I was taking this fight seriously, you'd be dead by now."

"I think I'd pay heed to his words," Cottonmouth suggested. He finally had managed to get his boot on.

"Stay out of this, you damn hog-hauler!" The ETMF man got to his feet and assumed the classic boxer's stance, shuffling toward Barry.

Barry kicked him on the kneecap and clubbed him on the neck with a balled fist as the driver went down.

"Driver," Barry told him, "I don't want to hurt you. Let's just call this off before you make me mad."

A crowd had gathered and several drivers stepped in and pulled the ETMF man to his feet. His eyes looked glazed.

"That's it," a driver said. "It's over. You gonna get hurt bad if you keep this up."

"Suits the hell outta me," the ETMF man agreed.

"Put some ice on that knee," Barry told him. "Keep it from stiffening up."

"You a wahoo, boy," Cottonmouth said, stepping forward and extending his hand. Barry shook it. "What's your handle?"

"Dog," Barry told him.

"You two gonna kiss each other?" Kate asked, disgust in her voice.

Barry looked at her. "Miss, has anybody ever told you that you're a little troublemaker?"

"Has anybody ever told you to go get fucked!" she hollered at him, then whirled around and marched toward the truck stop restaurant.

"Kate!" Cottonmouth yelled, stopping her. "Tell Big Joe I'll be in soon as I drop this load off in Beaumont. That is, if he still wants to hire me."

"He does. And bring hotshot there with you. That is, if he's got the balls to drive for a real outfit."

Barry smiled at her. "You'd be surprised what I can drive, Spitfire."

"You probably couldn't drive a vacuum cleaner around a livin' room!" She marched off into the truck stop.

"Kate Sherman," Cottonmouth said. "She's really something, ain't she?"

Barry just looked at him. He reserved comment.

"Rods that big Kenworth up and down the highways better than most men. Been with Rivers Trucking ever since she was a kid. One hundred and ten percent loyal to Big Joe. She likes you, too, Dog."

"*Likes* me!" Barry almost shouted the words. "What the hell would she do if she disliked me—shoot me?"

"Probably," Cottonmouth drawled. "She does carry a gun in her boot."

4

"I-7," Jackson told Barry and Lieutenant Cutter over breakfast the next morning. "One man was killed when you slapped the car off the road. Two were, we guess, pretty badly injured. That's based on the amount of blood in the car. The dead man was left. The two injured were probably taken to a doctor with IRA ties."

"Then this I-7 has a strong network in this country," Barry said. Statement, not a question.

"Oh, absolutely." Jackson was emphatic on that point. "As does the Islamic Army, the Bader-Meinhof gang, the Red Brigade—you name some terrorist group, and you'll find support for it somewhere in America. And a hell of a lot of support for the PLO."

"What's the word on leaks from the SST drivers?" Cutter asked.

"Nothing. A stone wall. But the SST drivers who were just about fifteen minutes behind you the other night"—he looked at Barry—"have all been reassigned. It was done quietly so as not to tip their hand. For the next few months, they'll be hauling retired weapons, taking them to the scrap pile. It's routine; all SST drivers do it at one time or another."

"Now what do we do?" Barry asked.

"You'll be hauling real weapons, M-16s, to the docks in New York City, for shipment overseas. We've deliberately let it leak about your cargo. So heads up, you're going to be hit."

"I'm not going to play this by any legal rules," Barry warned the government man. "Let's get that settled right now. I'm carte blanche on anything I do. Those were the terms of my agreement."

Jackson looked pained. He shifted his eyes to Cutter, then back to Barry. "We'd like to get enough on some people for convictions, Dog."

"Screw convictions. I intend to give them convictions with a bullet right between the eyes. Tell your legal department to stay the hell out of our way."

Jackson dropped his eyes. He knew Barry called the shots. That was the deal that had been made. And the administration that had made the deal was going to be in charge for a long time. Presidents might change, but the policy would not.

Jackson had been there. He recalled the conversation word for word: "Country has gone to hell, Barry," the President had said. "We're slowly bringing the nation back to dead center, but the liberals are fighting us tooth and claw all the way. We're losing some ground, gaining in some other areas. You might be able to help. Are you interested?"

"Do I have a choice?"

"Yes," the Man was quick to reply. "You hear me out. Then, if you're not interested, you're suddenly located in a hospital where you've been in a coma for months."

Barry listened. Smiled occasionally.

When the President was finished, Barry said, "I call the shots. I don't play by any rules. Person needs killing, I kill them. Courts turn loose a scumbag, if I'm close, he's dead. I am on my own. I am judge, jury, and executioner. Sometimes I might be called on to assist the government. That's fine. Just keep the social-moaners and weepers away from me."

The President had smiled. Made Jackson uncomfortable as hell.

The Man had said, "You will never see me again. I never heard of you. Your contact is Weston or Jackson. I never want to hear from you."

"Fine with me."

"You get out of control, and you're dead within twenty-four hours."

"I understand."

"You won't reconsider and have a partner?"

"I have a partner?"

"Oh? Who?"

"Dog."

He had shaken the President's hand. "Glad to have you with us, Barry."

"Call me Dog."

Jackson mentally shook himself and looked into the cold hunter/stalker/killer eyes of Barry Rivera—The Dog. "It's your show, Dog."

He stood up and walked out of the room.

Cutter leaned back in her chair and looked at Barry. "Man . . . just who in the hell are you, anyway? You just spoke to one of the top Treasury people like he was dirt under your boots."

"Jackson and I have to clear the air every now and then. We get along. Although that's hard to tell at times." He pushed back his chair. "Let's go to work, Cutter."

She smiled at him. "Yes, sir, boss!"

The smile was not returned. Hers faded on her face when he said, "Call me Dog."

They rolled out on a crisp October morning. Barry and Cutter in the lead truck. Ready and Smooth in the rocking chair. Frenchy and Mustard in the drag. It had not taken the instructors long to hone down the drivers. They had just spent three of the most brutal weeks of their lives. They had been awakened at four in the morning; they didn't see a bed until ten at night. For three weeks they did not walk anywhere. They ran all the time. Seemed to them they even ran in their sleep. And some of them did, legs jerking from exhaustion.

The Air Commando instructors had not turned out trained killers, not in three weeks, but they had taught the men what they could of self-defense and combat situations.

Barry and Cutter watched from the sidelines, but always ran with the other drivers, and stayed with them every waking hour.

A team was being formed.

Special radios had been installed in the trucks: military frequencies with scramblers.

They rolled east, fully loaded with M-16s and M-60 machine guns.

Cutter took the first trick at the wheel.

Dog was on the floor of the big walk-in custom sleeper. He was happy to once more be on the road.

"What did your people say about when we might be hit?" Barry asked.

"They couldn't get any intel on it. But it's almost always at night. Since we'll be out of the desert in a few hours, they'll probably try to take us out between Oklahoma City and St. Louis. I'm guessing when we get in the Ozarks. That's the way I'd do it."

"You've done this before?"

"In Europe, working with various police and military units."

"They do it differently over there, huh?"

"Much differently. The military and the police, in most of those countries, are not forbidden by law from working together. Spain and Germany are the best to work in."

"We picked up a tail," Frenchy radioed. "It's firm. Dark blue late-model Chevy. Four men in it."

The convoy was rolling at a steady 60 mph. It was odd that the car did not pass.

Cutter picked up the mike. "That'll be just one of several teams. I doubt they'll try anything in daylight, but you never know about these people."

"Ten-four."

"A second car is laying back," Ready radioed. "I seen it

when we come out of that last curve. It's back a good half mile. Dark blue or black. I couldn't tell."

"That's probably the second team. What we call a throwaway team," Cutter radioed. "The trick is they hope we'll worry about that team and fail to pick up on it when that Chevy pulls off and another team takes it place. This time probably ahead of us."

"Wrong," Barry said bitterly. "They're going to try us in broad open daylight." He had been looking out his window, watching a dot in the sky become larger.

"That's crazy!" Cutter said.

"Helicopter coming up fast from the south," he told her, then grabbed up his mike. "Heads up. Watch that damn chopper coming from the south."

The convoy was about sixty miles west of Tucumcari.

"Exit off!" Barry shouted. "Now. Let's take the fight to them!" He repeated the orders to the others.

Cutter hit the exit ramp too fast and had to stand on the brakes to avoid rolling when the ramp merged with a secondary road. She cut south, on a beat-up country road.

"That move blew their minds, Dog!" Frenchy yelled into his mike. "Caught 'em completely by surprise."

The helicopter had changed flight direction, the pilot confused by the sudden change in tactics of those on the ground. Barry could see a man sitting with a rifle in his hands.

Barry stuck his M-16 out the window and began letting the lead fly. The canopy of the chopper spiderwebbed and the pilot swerved away, content to let the ground personnel handle it from here on in.

Barry pointed to a broad intersection just ahead. "Turn it around there, Cutter. When you get it turned around, stay in the middle of the road and ram them." He radioed back to the others what he intended to do and then jumped from the seat and fitted Dog into a special harness, securing one end to a chrome O-ring on the sleeper wall. Barry got back in his seat just as Cutter was taking a wide swing and heading back.

"I wondered what that ring was for," Cutter shouted, over the roaring of the modified Cummins. "I thought you might be into leather and handcuffs!"

"That might be fun," Barry yelled. "You bring it up again when we're out of this!"

She smiled at him. "You might need handcuffs to handle me, Dog."

"Anytime you feel up to it, Cutter."

She laughed and shifted gears.

The driver of the Chevy had panic written all over his face as he realized what was coming at him and what was going to happen to him if he didn't do something and do it right the first time.

He just didn't act fast enough. The armor-plated and steel-reinforced front of the Kenworth caught the car just as the driver elected to turn. The massive reinforced bumper knocked the car off the road and flipped it rolling, just as the second car slid to a halt, the occupants spilling out, automatic weapons in their hands.

"Roll over them!" Barry shouted. "Goddamnit, do it!"

Cutter shifted and pedaled the metal. A terrorist was caught between the bumper of the Kenworth and the parked car. The bumper hit him stomach-high and crushed the life from him. The scream of metal against roadway was shrill in the autumn air combined with the roaring of the big Cummins, it drowned out the screaming of the other man who was caught under the wheels of the big rig and dragged to his death.

Barry grabbed for his mike. "Shut 'em down and come out firing!" he ordered.

He was out the door and on the ground before Cutter even brought the big rig to a complete halt.

Lining up one redheaded, freckle-faced man, Barry cut the legs out from under him and saw one kneecap shatter under the M-16 fire. Cutter was firing her weapon from the cab of the truck and the other drivers were rocking and rolling with automatic fire.

The helicopter was circling, but safely out of range.

The firefight was hot and intense, but the terrorists had been demoralized and thrown completely off guard by the actions of the drivers. In less than two minutes, the fight was over and the helicopter was a fading black dot in the sky. Hauling ass.

Barry glanced over at Cutter. Hell of a woman. She felt his eyes and met them.

"Those radios are repeaters, aren't they, Cutter?"

"Yes. Reading your mind, I'll contact Kirtland and get a team out here."

"Fine. Have the state police seal off that exit we used. I don't want anybody in here."

She nodded her head and climbed back up into the cab.

"Report!" Barry called.

"We're all okay!" Mustard yelled.

"Got a couple of live ones over here!" Ready called, standing over two moaning terrorists.

"And this one looks like an A-rab," Smooth said. "He's called me some dirty names, too."

"He'll be calling me more than that before I'm through with the son of a bitch," Barry muttered. Raising his voice, he called, "Bring the live ones over here."

Cutter was climbing down as the wounded terrorists were dragged to Barry's rig.

"What are you going to do, Barry?" she asked.

"Question this bastard."

She appeared nervous about that and Barry picked up on it. Asked her about it.

"I would rather you waited until my team got here."

"Why?"

"We're on U.S. soil, Barry."

"Yes," Barry told her. "And I intend to see that it *remains* U.S. soil."

He turned to Frenchy. "Get his driver's license for me, please."

An international driver's license and a passport. "The asshole thinks he has diplomatic immunity," Barry said. "He's some sort of Iranian attaché."

Cutter looked at the visa. "Barry, he *does* have diplomatic immunity."

"Not with me." That made Cutter even more nervous. Barry knelt down beside the man. "Who tipped you that we were hauling this route?"

The Iranian, only slightly wounded, spat in Barry's face. Barry stood up, wiped the spittle from his face, then kicked the terrorist between the legs.

The man screamed and rolled on the ground.

Cutter had regained her composure and was leaning up against the trailer, her arms folded under her breasts. This was the Dog's show. She had been ordered not to interfere.

Whatever Barry did to the man, she'd seen worse in Europe. From terrorist's bombs and bullets.

"I asked you a question, camel-humper. Who tipped you?"

The Iranian glared at Barry with eyes filled with both pain and hate.

Barry smiled at him. "All right, partner. If that's the way you want to play the game, suits me just fine." He looked at Frenchy. "Couple of you boys wedge his right ankle under the outside tire of the trailer and hold him there."

The Iranian started screaming and kicking.

"What are you going to do?" the red-haired, freckle-faced man asked, a lilting brogue to his voice.

Barry looked at him. "I'm going to see how Abdullah here likes life with his ankles crushed."

"This is America," the Irishman said. "Here, you have justice and courts and laws and procedures one must follow."

"No," Barry softly corrected him. "Not *here.*" He pointed to the ground. "Here, you got the Dog!"

5

All things taken into consideration, it was really quite unpleasant for the Iranian terrorist. But he talked. After one ankle was crushed under the tires of the big rig, and after he was brought back to consciousness, he began talking so fast it was difficult for Barry and Cutter to keep up. But Cutter's cassette/recorder got it all. She also committed it to memory and jotted down telephone numbers, knowing she would have to turn the tape over to her team leader.

While Cutter was taping the Iranian's statements, Barry turned his attention to the red-haired, freckle-faced man, who had remained impassive during the Iranian's painful incentive toward talking.

Now he said, "Unconstitutional, illegal, barbaric, and quite un-American."

"You're breaking my heart," Barry told him. "I'm almost overcome with emotion. I want the location of your safe houses and the leaders of cells within the United States."

"You must be mad!"

"Actually, no."

The face of the terrorist was sweat-shiny and his eyes were dulled from the pain of the wounds in his legs. "I demand to see a doctor. That is my constitutional right under American law."

"All right," Barry told him. "Give me the name of the nearest doctor sympathetic to your so-called cause, and we'll get you to him, or her, promptly."

"You are a rotten son of a bitch!" the terrorist cursed him.

"You're the one lying on the ground bleeding and hurting, not me," Barry reminded him.

The wounded terrorist again cursed Barry.

"Drag that other one over here," Barry told Mustard. He turned to Cutter. "You familiar with this kid-looking punk?"

She nodded her head. "Darin Grady. He's the one responsible for blowing up that department store in England. The blast that killed all those civilians."

Barry squatted down beside the young man. "O'Grady, is it now, my boy?"

Darin spat at Barry, the spittle plopping in the sand by Barry's boot.

Barry cut his eyes to Smooth. "You check his wounds?"

"He's not bad hurt. Probably not as bad as he's gonna be hurt," he added.

"I find your actions very reprehensible," Darin said. "And I demand prompt medical attention and legal representation."

Barry laughed at him. "When a leprechaun appears on my shoulder, punk. I want information, and I want it quickly."

"Or you'll torture me?"

"If I have to."

"Then you're no better than you claim us to be."

"Wrong. I don't plant bombs that kill indiscriminately." Barry stood up and kicked the man in the mouth.

Cutter winced as teeth bounced across the sand and Darin Grady screamed in pain.

The other drivers had walked away at a wave of Barry's hand.

Barry had reached toward the folding knife encased in leather on his belt when the sound of helicopters stopped his hand.

"They're ours," Cutter announced.

The choppers settled down, kicking up dirt and sand. Jackson ran to the scene. He paused at the front of Barry's truck, paling at the sight of blood and bits of bone and guts clinging to the grill and bumper.

The Air Force Special Operations team quickly assessed the scene and stayed back, their faces impassive.

Jackson knelt down beside the moaning Iranian and spoke with him briefly. He rose to his feet and faced Barry, anger in his eyes.

"You fucked up, Dog! You realize that with what you've done, we can never take any of these people into an open court of law."

"So what?" Barry stood his ground. He pointed to the nearly unconscious Iranian. "That one spilled his guts. Cutter has it on tape." He pointed to Darin. "And I was just about to get some information out of this one."

"I protest!" Darin cried. "I demand to see a doctor and be treated as a prisoner of war under the terms of the Geneva Convention."

Blood was leaking out of his ruined mouth.

"Shut up, asshole!" Barry told him. "The Geneva Convention doesn't apply to terrorists."

"That's it, Dog!" Jackson's voice was sharp. "I take it from this point."

Barry walked to him. "Jackson, you're gonna screw it all up. I told you to keep the legal shit out of this operation."

"Damn it, Barry." He pointed to the terrorist with the crushed and mangled ankle. "That's an Iranian diplomat. I don't know how in the hell we're going to handle this situation."

"I do. Put him back in that car and burn it. He had an accident. End of report. Let the Iranians protest all they want. It won't do them any good. And leave Darin Grady to me."

Jackson looked to Cutter for support. He didn't get it. She met his eyes with a bleak stare.

He looked at the Special Operations team. One of them was eating a candy bar.

"I missed breakfast," he explained.

"Get these people loaded up in the helicopters," Jackson ordered. "We've got to get them medical attention."

"You're making a mistake, Jackson," Barry told him.

"I made a mistake by agreeing with the President to allow a person like you to even exist."

"Jackson?"

"What, Dog?"

"I always suspected you were a bleeding liberal at heart."

The Treasury man flushed. "No, Barry. I'm just a man who believes in operating within the boundaries of human decency and within the framework of the law."

"And that is exactly the reason why we are going to eventually lose the fight with terrorism."

"Deliver your load, Dog. I'll be in touch."

"What do you figure the odds are of them hitting us again this trip?" Barry asked Cutter.

"Personally, I don't think they'll risk it. But as I've said before, you never can figure a terrorist group. They'll do the unexpected. But one thing is for sure: we're on the top of their hit list now."

"Jackson is going to blow it," Barry predicted.

"I'm afraid you're right. But you have to understand his position, Barry: he's got to go the legal route. He had absolutely no choice in the matter."

"From now on, Jackson does not figure in anything we do, Cutter. He's out of the picture."

They rode on for a few miles in silence, Barry at the wheel. Tucumcari was a few miles behind them, the Texas border just ahead.

Cutter broke the silence of the road. "I am absolutely baffled as to how Jackson thinks he's going to keep this out of the press."

"By making a deal with the Iranian government."

"With Khomeini? Jesus! You don't make deals with that nut."

"He's going to try. And fail."

"And the press is going to blow it wide open."

"Yep."

She shook her head. "I will never understand why this government ever allowed Khomeini to come to power."

"Because when Khomeini was living in Paris, we didn't have enough guts to burn him. Certain officials in France were willing to turn their backs, allowing us to hit Khomeini. Other governments were willing to help us ease the Shah out and install a more moderate government in Iran, but we didn't, and that's a fact. I was an arms dealer and consultant back then, shuttling back and forth between Europe and America. The Europeans were so pissed-off about Khomeini many were practically livid."

"Why didn't they burn him?"

"Politics. Only two nations make decisions that will shape international politics, Cutter. You know that. Russia and the U.S. Discounting Third World nations, of course. The other nations can make minor decisions. Anything else and we are almost always consulted."

Barry pulled over at a co-op and weighed his load, then the convoy was once more on the road, rolling eastward at a steady 60 mph.

"A successful arms dealer. An arms consultant. And now you're driving a truck and operating as a gun for the government." She was stating fact, not asking questions.

"I fought the mob in New Orleans, Cutter. I fought traitors within our government. My wife was killed by a bomb that was meant for me. I was in a hospital for months. The man I used to be no longer exists. He's dead. Buried. This Kenworth is my home."

"A rolling court of law, the driver judge, jury, and executioner."

"Your words, Cutter. Not mine."

She slipped back into the sleeper. "I'm going to take a nap."

"I'll wake you in a couple of hours. We'll stop then for lunch."

Dog jumped up into the recently vacated seat and stared out the window at the passing landscape.

Barry missed Cutter's company. And that was not a feeling he enjoyed.

When Cutter again slid back into the front seat, she was startled to see a Welcome to Oklahoma sign looming up on the right.

"You might have awakened me, Barry. You must be tired."

"We have to weigh right up here. You can take the wheel then. It is just a short run across this part of Texas."

"I didn't think I was that tired," Cutter remarked, glancing at her watch.

"It was a fairly interesting morning." Barry said that with a smile.

She looked at him to see if he was kidding.

"It's a good thing we hosed off all that gore from the front of the truck. Seeing that might have shook the weight watchers up some."

"For a fact. Damn sure shook Jackson up." The weight watcher behind the glass told him he was okay and Barry pulled ahead, to wait for the others.

"Have you heard anything on the news?"

"Not a peep. I imagine the President was the first to be informed. And knowing him, he's probably contemplating nailing Jackson's hide to the barn door."

Cutter was curious about that 'knowing him' bit. But she did not pursue it. "Jackson's between a rock and a hard place, Barry."

They changed places and Cutter made herself comfortable behind the wheel, adjusting the seat to her liking.

"You hungry?" Barry asked.

"Ravenous."

"Next place you see, pull over. I could do with a bite myself."

"How do we work that? I mean, somebody has to stay with the trucks."

"You and I will eat last. Rain, hail, snow, whatever, we've

got to be outside guarding against somebody planting a bomb on us."

"Then I'd better get some rain gear up ahead."

"That would be a good idea."

Ready and Frenchy and Smooth and Mustard went inside to eat, leaving Barry and Cutter to guard the trucks. Neither one of them anticipated any move against them this quickly after the shoot-out, and they were correct in that. They may as well have been guarding a tomb. No one came near the rigs.

Barry and Cutter ate and the convoy was back on the road in forty-five minutes.

They rolled on, taking the northerly route: Oklahoma City to St. Louis—they rolled through there just after dawn. St. Louis to Indianapolis. From Indy a grueling shot over to Philly and then a short hop to New York.

They met some bitching at the docks. But none of them paid any attention to it. There was always some bitching at New York City docks. Finally a man from the military showed up, with the right ID, and the shipment was signed over to be unloaded.

They had screwed off half a day at the docks.

And it was another half day before they got unloaded.

Barry had no orders, no idea where to catch up with Jackson, and no inclination to call him anyway.

Cutter did not like the smile on Barry's face and said as much.

"What the hell have you got on your mind, Barry?" she asked.

"I know you gave that tape recording to Jackson, but how much of what that jerk told you do you remember?"

"All of it."

"Remember the addresses he gave you in New York?"

"Certainly." She looked at him. "Barry! . . ."

"Come on, Cutter. Let's go raise a little hell!"

They had driven away from the city, over into New Jersey and found a motel that had the space to accept their rigs. Barry and a very reluctant Meri Cutter would go back into the city after a bath and change of clothing. The others would stay at the motel, taking shifts guarding the rigs and watching after Dog.

Barry arranged for a rental car and it was delivered to the motel.

He changed into sport coat and slacks, low quarter shoes, all dark, with a dark turtleneck sweater.

He wore a Beretta 9mm, sixteen shot, in a shoulder holster, and a .25-caliber Beretta, loaded with custom-made hollow noses, in an ankle holster. He packed lots of other goodies into a large attaché case and waited for Cutter to make her appearance.

It was worth the wait.

She looked like a flat million bucks. The night was cool and she wore a custom-made leather jacket, waist length. Barry knew the name of the design. It came to him. Bolero. Like Barry, she had dressed in dark clothing. From her boots to her shirt.

"You carrying?" he asked.

"One here." She patted the side of her jacket. "And one in my boot."

"You ready?"

"What's in the briefcase?"

"Things that go bump in the night."

She rolled her eyes. "Oh, well. I'm still young enough to find another career."

Barry opened the door and bowed. "Shall we be off, my dear?"

"One of us is, for a fact."

"You drive."

"The age of chivalry is dead."

"Oh? Not really."

"Explain."

"I intend to let you cut the first throat tonight."

"The man is so sensitive to a woman's needs."

"Thank you."

"Get in the damn car, Dog!"

6

"What was the guy's name who is ramrodding the operation?"

"Khaled."

"You familiar with him?"

She laughed, unpleasantly. "Everybody in the intelligence community knows about Khaled. He's on hit lists from half the countries in the world."

"And he's in New York? Is that what that jerk said?"

"That's what he said. But Barry, if Khaled wasn't notified within minutes after the strike went down the other day, he's shifted locations. Bet on it."

"All right, level with me. I've seen you making phone calls. Your people told you something."

"We're hot, Barry. There is a big diplomatic flap in the wind. I didn't tell you because I was ordered not to tell you."

"Well, hell, Cutter! I figured out there was going to be an explosion at State."

"I learned about thirty minutes ago that there is a one hundred-thousand-dollar price tag on your head. And going up daily. The man called the Dog is so hot I could burn my finger just touching you."

Barry grinned at her. "Work now, Cutter. Romance later."

She called him a very ugly name. But she was smiling as she did.

* * *

She parked the car in a secured area and from that point they took taxis. They chatted lightly, like tourists, oohhing and aahhing at the crowds on this Saturday night, craning their necks to gawk at the tall, lighted buildings that stretched upward toward the sky.

Twice they changed cabs; then, sure they were not followed, they stepped into a subway entry and bought a pocketful of tokens; should they have to take a bus, the buses also take the subway tokens.

They surfaced in a quiet residential neighborhood.

"Nice neighborhood," Barry remarked, his eyes taking in the lack of trash on the street and no roaming gangs of street punks.

"One would never think this would be the headquarters of a terrorist organization, right?"

"And you people knew all along where to find this Khaled?"

"He doesn't stay here often. But to answer your question: yes. We knew. The agency knew. Several other intelligence organizations knew. As to why we didn't give the authorities that information? We didn't want him to be tried publicly. We didn't want him extradited. We wanted him dead. Period. But we had to work carefully and never got a chance to burn him. We mustn't violate his constitutional rights, you know?"

"Oh, quite." Barry's reply was dry. He glanced at her in the glow of the street lamps. "And you think he's gone from here?"

"We know he's gone. He's somewhere in Chicago. But several of his top aides are still here." She pointed to the second floor of the building. "Right up there."

"Any children up there?"

"We don't think so."

"That's not good enough for me."

"Nor for us. People like Khaled are smart, Barry. Just like Darin Grady is smart. They know that Americans are not going to cold-bloodedly kill kids. Bombs falling out of the sky are one thing. The pilots never know. But people like Khaled and Darin know—for an absolute fact—that we won't wire a car to blow if there is even the remotest chance a child will be caught up in it. That's one of our many weak points—if you want to call that a weak point—and terrorists worldwide know it."

"But they don't mind killing kids?"

"That is correct."

"So you feel there might be kids in that apartment?"

"Fifty-fifty chance, yes."

"Would you know one of Khaled's aides if he stepped out to the street?"

"Oh, yes. There are two living up there. A PLO member who calls himself Jabal—real name unknown—and a Lebanese terrorist who goes by the name of Gibran—real name unknown. Their girlfriends are also terrorists. A German girl with ties to the Bader-Meinhof gang, and an Irish girl who works closely with I-7." She described the four of them.

"You know all this, yet can't move against them?"

"Politics, Barry. They have committed no crimes in this country, and no crimes anywhere else under the names they are now using."

"But you know their names are false?"

"Certainly. So does the State Department. So does the FBI. And certain members of the NYPD do, too. But they all have some immunity, being connecting with the U.N."

Barry cursed.

Cutter smiled. "All right, we're here. Now what?"

"Wonder what would happen if I threw a rock through that front window?"

"Oh, they'd call the police! After all, every one of them is a good, law-abiding visitor to this country."

Barry studied the front door. "Electrically operated from each apartment?"

"Oh, yes."

"Some sort of alarm on the basement door?"

"Oh, yes."

"Let's go in."

"I thought you'd never ask."

They slipped into the darkness of the alley and made their way around to the back of the apartment building. Barry smiled. Somebody had wedged the spring-loaded fire escape ladder to the alley floor.

"Kids, probably," Cutter said.

"Bless their little hearts. Come on."

They slipped up the ladder, cautiously making their way past the second floor. At the third floor, Barry tried the window. Open. Smiling, he slipped inside, Cutter right behind him. They found the stairs and silently descended to the second floor. On the landing, Barry took out a .22-caliber auto-loader from his briefcase and screwed a silencer onto the tapped barrel.

Cutter held open one side of her leather jacket. Her .380 had already been fitted for silent operation.

She touched his arm. "We have no way of getting anyone out of here for questioning, Barry," she said in a whisper.

A nice way of saying the apartment was about to be turned into a slaughterhouse.

He nodded and they moved silently up the carpeted hall. Cutter stopped him at an apartment door. She looked at him and formed a question mark in the air with one finger.

Barry smiled and then almost scared her out of her fashion jeans by simply reaching out and knocking on the door.

Footsteps from inside. "Who is it?" The voice was low and just audible coming through the thick door.

"I have the Dog," Barry said.

Cutter rolled her eyes in utter disbelief at Barry's audacity and pressed herself against the wall, to remain unseen when the door to the apartment opened.

Barry recognized the man as Gibran as he peeked out the small crack in the door. The chain remained in place, offering only a few inches of space between door and jamb.

"I know nothing about anything called a Dog," Gibran said.

"Then where do I collect my money?"

The man hesitated. Made up his mind. What a coup this would be. He could rise high up in the organization if he could produce the faceless but deadly Dog. "Where do you have this person?"

Barry smiled. "Outside. In the car. He's drugged."

Gibran paled. He cut his eyes and said something in a language Barry could not understand. Reaching up, he slid the chain free and opened the door. "Quickly, inside."

Barry stepped into the room, his eyes sweeping the area. One other man and two women. Cutter had described them all perfectly. He lifted his right hand and shot Gibran twice in the chest, the huffing hollow noses expanding and driving into the terrorist's heart. He was conscious of Cutter coming in behind him, moving swiftly. Her .380 chugged softly and the women, both of them sitting on the couch slumped to one side, their faces and chests staining with blood.

Barry's .22 coughed twice more, just as the second man in the room, Jabal, was coming up with a pistol. The slugs turned him around and he sank to the carpet. Barry finished the terrorist with a single shot to the side of his head.

"I'll fan the bedrooms," Cutter said. "You take this room. Anything with words on it, take it, no matter what the language."

"Check for kids."

She nodded.

Barry walked to the door and closed it, making sure the lock caught.

Ignoring the bodies, he swiftly fanned the room finding several sheets of paper written in what he supposed was Arabic. Those went into his jacket pocket. He found a diary in the middle drawer of a small desk. Nothing more.

He turned as Cutter entered the room stuffing a wad of papers into an inside pocket of her jacket.

"Kids?" Barry asked.

She shook her head. "Kids' clothing. But no sign that any child ever lived here for any length of time."

"Let's go."

Cutter checked the hall. Clear. She looked back at Barry. "Out the front way?"

He nodded.

They walked out of the apartment building boldly and several blocks later stepped into a subway entry. They caught a cab that took them midtown and then another cab and finally a bus.

They had not been followed.

The convoy, running empty, rolled out at seven o'clock the next morning.

"Goddamn you!" Jackson yelled through the phone into Barry's ear. "We were just about to move against those people. You've just thrown gasoline onto a fire, Dog!"

Barry had called Jackson from a pay phone at a truck stop in Pennsylvania.

"I don't know what you're talking about, Jackson. We dropped our loads at the docks and waited for twenty-four hours for orders from you. Spent the night at a motel in New Jersey. You can check it out. Now what do you mean about my throwing gasoline on a fire?"

Jackson sputtered for a moment and then calmed himself. "Don't you read the papers or listen to TV news, Barry?"

"Jackson, we've been on the road. Deadheading to nowhere. When the hell am I going to have time to read a newspaper or watch TV?"

"All right, all right! You did it. I can't prove it. You won't admit it. So to hell with it. Certain people in government say thank you for it. I don't. But I don't count."

"You're babbling, Jackson. Are you coming down with something?"

"Yeah. Rabies, probably. I have bad news, Dog."

"What else is new?"

Jackson sighed. "Darin Grady escaped from federal custody."

"You son of a bitch!"

"Look, Dog . . ."

"No, *you* look! Darin can describe me. The truck I'm driving. He saw Cutter and Smooth and Mustard and Ready and Frenchy. You've signed the death warrants for them all."

"It couldn't be helped."

"Oh, yeah? Yeah, it could have been helped, Jackson. And you know it. So from now on, you don't give me orders concerning my little war. You assign me loads, and that's it. Is that clear?"

"Funny. I got the same message about five hours ago."

"I don't doubt that a bit. And I can guess where you got the message. Next load, Jackson?"

"Head to Randolph AFB. San Antonio. Cutter's team is there. Captain Barnett wants to talk with her. Orders will be there for you."

"Fine. Now how in the hell did Grady bust loose?"

"It appears that someone in government got to I-7 and tipped off Grady's location. The Air Force lost four men, Dog. NCO's. Good security men. Certain people within the Air Force are highly pissed."

"No kidding! Do you blame them?"

No reply.

"Any idea who in government rolled over?"

"We have some names."

"And. . . ?"

"We're going to let them play out their string."

"And. . . ?"

"Then you can take care of it, Dog."

"Thank you."

"I was wrong, Dog. I admit it. We don't see eye to eye, but I won't—or I'll try very hard—not to interfere with you after this."

"It would be appreciated. Why the change of heart?"

"You really haven't read a newspaper or listened to the news, have you?"

"I told you I haven't." That much was true.

"All right. There were multiple terrorist strikes all over Europe last night. Probably in retaliation for the failed attempt on your convoy out in New Mexico. It wasn't for the murders of those . . . people in New York. We've put a lid on that. But when the terrorist community learns of it, watch out." Jackson sighed. "A hundred and sixty people died, Dog. In one night. Ireland, England, France, Germany, Spain. So far, the count shows thirty children were murdered. And they haven't finished the count, yet."

Jackson hung up.

Barry walked slowly back to his crew and waved them around him. He told them about the escape of Darin Grady, and the news about the terrorist strikes. And about the kids.

Cutter's face hardened. That was her only show of emotion.

The men shifted uncomfortably on the blacktop parking lot, Ready saying, "How about our kids, Barry?"

"I'd say they were in danger. Your wives more than your kids. And I probably don't have to explain that."

"Me and Sally got married right after I got out of the Army. I would not take kindly to anything happening to her. No matter how slight."

Barry felt Cutter's eyes on him, and knew she was thinking about what he'd said: 'My wife was killed by a bomb meant for me.'

He said, "If you want out, now is the time to say it. You get in any deeper, and it'll be too late. To tell you the truth, it probably is too late now."

"That is probably more like it," Mustard remarked. "I figure we're all marked men by now."

"What the hell are these people fightin' for?" Smooth asked. He tossed the question out to anyone who might want to pick it up.

"They claim they're fighting for freedom," Cutter told him. "Among other things."

"They kill little innocent kids and they say they're fighting for freedom?" Frenchy asked. "That's dumber than Vietnam. I got shot twice over there and still ain't figured out why."

It was just too good to pass up. "Why?" Mustard looked at him. "Hell, you probably stuck your big ass up in the air is why!"

Frenchy looked pained. "That ain't what I meant, you buzzard-lookin' thing."

"Buzzard-lookin'! Was I you, I sure wouldn't be callin' nobody ugly. You so ugly I bet your momma had to tie a sweet potato around your neck to get the hogs to play with you!"

"Me, ugly? Compared to you I'm a regular Paul Newman. Only reason your wife stays with you is 'cause your face scares the kids so bad they don't misbehave none. What do you do for a hobby, haunt graveyards?"

Barry and Cutter walked away from the group. Cutter asked, "I wonder if all that insulting means they're staying."

"That bunch? Sure, they're sticking. You couldn't pry them away from this now."

"What else did Jackson say?"

"Your team leader wants to talk to you."

"I just bet he does."

"Could you make any sense out of those papers we got back at the apartment?"

"Yes, but they won't do us much good. They were all outdated materials. It'll give us a few more names with no locations." She smiled. "You know I've already called most of it in."

He nodded. "You do your job and I'll do mine."

"We worked pretty well together back there, Barry."

He had to admit that they had. "I also got the impression that wasn't your first cold kill."

"They do things differently in Europe, Barry. They don't believe that everything the government does in the national interest is the business of the people. I tend to agree with them."

"I couldn't agree more." He looked at her and waggled his eyebrows. "Wanna go boogie-woogie tonight, Cutter?"

She laughed. "We'll be boogie-woogieing all right. Bebopping down to Texas."

"What a party-pooper!"

"Hey!" Ready hollered, confirming what Barry had guessed. "Let's get this show on the road. We got a load to pick up."

7

Ten hours later they pulled into a truck stop outside of Nashville and climbed down from their rigs. Barry stayed with Cutter with the rigs while the others went in to shower and change into fresh clothing and get something to eat. The night was clear and cold and the heavens were pocked with stars. Diamonds set in black velvet. They did a walkaround of the rigs, one going one way, the other the opposite direction.

They met at the rear of the trailers and leaned up against them, talking.

"Ever married, Cutter?"

She shook her head, then realized that he could not see the gesture in the night. "No. Never even came close."

He looked at her. "Beautiful woman like you? Damn, that's hard to believe."

"You may not have noticed, Barry, but I am not exactly a small lady."

"Oh, I noticed. Believe that."

"There have been men in my life." She grimaced. "The wrong types of men, unfortunately. These hotshot macho boys give me a pain in the butt. The types who quote/unquote 'want to make a real woman out of me.' Then there is the real male chauvinist pig type. And, brother, don't ever even think the woods aren't filled with them. The types who think a woman's place is in the home."

"If you don't mind me saying it, you would have liked Kate."

"I don't mind it at all. That was your wife's name?"

"Yeah." The word was soft. "She could drive a rig like this one just as good as any man ever thought about doing. Then go put on a dress and dance until I hollered uncle."

"You miss her, don't you, Barry?"

"Yes."

"Have there been other women in your life since Kate?"

"One. For a very brief period. In Kentucky. Some months back."

"Any plans of ever going back and seeing her?"

"No."

"Any particular reason for that?"

"There is no point." He patted the trailer. "I told you: this rig is my home. I made a decision, and it was solely mine to make." He smiled in the night, his teeth flashing white against his tanned face. "What's your excuse, Cutter?"

"I guess the right man just hasn't come along."

Barry said nothing. He had a hunch she had found—or thought she had found—that right man. And he felt vibes from her. Good vibes. Vibes that told him she would be the one to stand beside him, through the good times and the bad.

But he knew that could never be.

"Keep looking, Cutter." He walked away, very conscious of her eyes on his back.

Barry's eyes popped open. He did not know what had awakened him; he had always been able to sleep as soundly in a moving truck as in a stationary bed, having been raised in the cab of a truck.

He looked at his watch. Three o'clock. He'd been asleep just about six hours, which was about all he ever slept at one stretch.

He slipped out of the bunk and pulled on his boots and

shirt. Dog bumped his head against Barry's leg, letting the man know he was on the floor and to keep his big feet off him.

Barry patted the animal on the head and slipped up front, into the passenger seat. Looking at Cutter in the glow of instrument lights, he felt a stirring. He fought it back.

"You were tired," Cutter said, not taking her eyes off the road.

"Yes. But I don't know what caused me to wake up like I did. A feeling that something was wrong."

"I've had that same feeling for the past fifteen minutes or so. I almost woke you up a couple of times."

"You should have. You talked to any of the others?"

"No."

Barry picked up the mike for the high-band military radio. "This is Dog. How's it looking in the drag?"

"I don't know." Frenchy. "At times I think we're being followed. Then the lights cut off. I can't tell if it's the same car that's behind me. But I got a hunch it is."

"I got a bad feelin'," Ready broke in. "I think we'd better stay heads up."

"Where the hell are we?" Barry asked Cutter.

"About halfway between Memphis and Little Rock. It's a good stretch of highway for an ambush."

He looked out the window and silently agreed with her. There was not a light to be seen. But how the hell would any terrorist group know the route they were taking? Not even Jackson knew that. But if someone placed just right in government knew where the convoy was when Barry contacted Jackson, and knew where they were heading, it would be relatively easy to figure out the route.

Had he told Jackson where he was when he talked with him? He thought back. Yeah, he had. That truck stop in Pennsylvania. And the logical route from there to San Antonio was the one they were taking.

Barry checked a highway mileage marker and then looked

at a map of Arkansas. "We've got about fifteen miles of nothing looking at us, Cutter. If something is going to go down, this is where it'll happen." He picked up his mike. "Everybody over in the left lane. Guards, window down and weapons at the ready. Heads up."

Barry picked up his Uzi and checked the clip. Full. Always set on full auto. Ready to rock and roll. He waited for someone to start the dance.

Barry looked up ahead, to an on-ramp, and smiled grimly. "They're getting smart, Cutter."

She had seen the big Peterbilt roaring off the ramp, its movement timed perfectly to intercept the convoy.

"Got a rig coming up behind fast!" Frenchy's voice came through the speaker.

"He's going to try to ram!" Cutter said.

Barry leaned out the window and gave the rogue 18-wheeler a full clip from the Uzi. The left-side mirror erupted in a shower of glass and metal, the sudden burst of fire startling the driver, giving Cutter time to pull up alongside of the rig. The man on the passenger side held what looked like a MAC-10 in his hands.

Barry slammed a fresh clip into the Uzi, jacked in a round, and emptied the weapon into the cab of the Peterbilt. In the glow of lights, Barry watched the driver's face explode, splattering the interior of the truck with blood and bone.

"Shut it down!" Barry yelled.

Cutter stood on the brakes, tires smoking.

The maverick 18-wheeler veered off to the left, running wide open and out of control. It cut across the left lane and disappeared out of sight, rolling across the median and landing upside down.

"Hammer down!" Barry yelled.

Cutter threw the coals to the rig, twin chrome stacks smoking and the engine roaring.

"Over in the right lane, Cutter!" He jerked up his mike and

keyed it. "Ready, Frenchy! Come on around us. You're paid to haul freight, not be heroes. We'll handle it."

"Now you look here, Dog!" Ready's voice yelled through the speaker.

"Do what I tell you, goddamnit. Come on, if those goddamn piles of junk you're driving will make it."

The SSTs were all almost identical, but no driver likes his rig insulted. In the mirror, Barry smiled as the drivers poured it on, coming up fast.

"Slow down, Cutter. Let them get around us and then we'll take out this other bastard."

Cutter eased off the pedal and Ready and Frenchy took the lead.

"It's us they want," Cutter said.

"I'm damn sure going to give them a chance to try their luck." Barry's words were formed around a grim smile.

Dog was lying on the floor of the sleeper, growling.

The terrorist 18-wheeler began closing with Barry's Kenworth.

"Now we get to see how you drive, Cutter." Barry told her. "Get in the center, straddle the line."

She swung the big rig into the center of the Interstate.

The rig behind them closed, sitting on their donkey.

They were rolling at seventy. Barry knew his rig, empty, would better a hundred mph. But he also knew that at any second they might come up on some four-wheeler, and he did not want to see any innocent people hurt.

A rig passed them on the other side of the Interstate, eastbound. "How's it lookin' over your shoulder, buddy?" the CB crackled.

"Haven't seen a thing since River City," Cutter answered calmly.

"You sound sweet."

"That's what my wife says."

The driver thought about that for a few seconds. "Your *wife?*"

"Yeah. She's in the bunk. We're gonna pull over in a few and get down to business."

"Well, the hell with you both! I'm gone! Good night!"

The radio went silent.

Barry's right-side mirror shattered under the impacting of automatic weapons fire, momentarily filling the air with tiny images of highway and lights as the glass showered.

Barry reached into his war bag and pulled out several grenades.

Cutter gave him a sharp look. "How much armament do you carry in this rig?"

Barry just grinned. "Pull over into the left lane. Let's see what he does."

She swung over, leaving the right-hand lane clear. The rogue 18-wheeler took the bait and swung over, attempting to pull up even with Barry and Cutter.

Barry pulled the pin and tossed the grenade out the window. It bounced off the road and exploded harmlessly on the grass by the shoulder.

Muttering low curses, Barry grabbed up another grenade and jerked the pin, holding the spoon down.

"Have you got a firm grip on that thing?" Cutter yelled, over the roar of the engine and the sounds of the exhaust and the wind coming in through Barry's open window.

"If I don't, it's sure gonna get messy in here!"

Either the driver of the rogue truck was traveling too fast to see the grenade as it exploded, or he was just plain stupid. Either way, he kept on trucking.

Barry released the spoon, counted, and tossed the pineapple out the window, tossing it as straight back as he could.

The grenade exploded just as it impacted with the front of the truck. He wasn't sure how much damage he had done, but the truck slewed to one side and pulled over onto the shoulder. One headlight was gone and it looked like the blast had torn one fender off, but Barry couldn't be sure.

"Do we go back and finish it?" Cutter asked.

Barry shook his head. "No. We need to get the hell gone from this area." He was thoughtful for a moment. "When we get to a rest area, pull over for a minute. I want to take off what's left of this shot-up mirror. We'll replace it outside of Little Rock. You arrange for the mirror. I'll call Jackson."

"You're bait, Barry." Jackson was blunt. "Pure and simple. You, Cutter, and the others. The price on your head just went up to a hundred and fifty thousand dollars. The news of Jabal and Gibran and the women broke just after I spoke with you."

"Who leaked it?"

"No leak on our part this time. The press was notified, we think, by Khaled's people."

"You think?"

"The press refuses to divulge their sources."

"Give me the reporter's name. I'll get it out of the son of a bitch!"

"I am sorely tempted to do just that. But, no. I was hoping you'd call in. You're too hot to handle real loads, Barry. And they know, somehow, you're San Antonio bound. So let's see if we can throw them off. Head for . . . wait a minute . . . yeah. Sheppard AFB at Wichita Falls. I'll advise Captain Barnett to meet you people there. That okay with you, Dog?"

"We're on our way."

A new mirror in place, the small convoy rolled out. They would head to Fort Smith, then Oklahoma City. From there, they would head south on 44 into Sheppard.

"Bait," Cutter said, emerging from the sleeper and sitting down. "I've been thinking about that." She looked out at the passing Oklahoma landscape.

"And. . . ?" Barry prompted.

"I like it."

"I'm riding with a crazy woman!"

"No. Think about it. The possibilities are endless."

"Yeah. For us to get our butts shot off?"

"That, yes. But also for us to shoot off some butts."

"I'm kidding with you, Cutter. Being bait is fine with me. But I'd like to get Frenchy and the others off the hook."

She looked at him. "But none of the rest of my team can drive a rig like this."

"We don't need them."

"We?"

"You and me, Cutter. We make a good team."

"You mean that, Barry?"

"Cutter and the Dog."

"I like it."

8

"I hate it!" Jackson said.

"So do I," Captain Barnett echoed.

"I've already spoken with SOCOM," Cutter said. "They like it. Orders are being cut right now. So it's settled. I ride with the Dog."

"You can't do it," Jackson said smugly. "It's against the law."

Barry looked at the man and laughed. "Jackson, that is the most asinine thing I have ever heard you say. I'm riding around the country killing people with the government's blessing, and you tell Cutter she can't ride with me because it's against the law!"

Jackson looked pained. "Barry, your cover is ripped enough without broadcasting what you do."

"Jackson," Barry said, looking at the Air Force Special Operations team. "These people have the highest national security clearance known to exist. My God, there must be five thousand or more truck drivers out there"—he waved his hand—"who know what I do, and fifty thousand more who suspect."

"Yes," Jackson agreed. "And that has caused some concern in very high quarters."

"And. . . ?"

Jackson shrugged his shoulders. "Only one person can stop you, Barry. And that person has no intention of ever doing so. Funds for what you are doing were set aside a long time before we ever even knew your name. Long before you actually came into the picture. Provisions for you were worked into the charter of . . . a certain organization." He sighed. "All right. All right. You and Lieutenant Cutter can't just hit the highways, running about willy-nilly. There have to be plans made. So"— he sat down wearily—"let's get to it."

"And let those truckers roll!" Cutter said with a laugh.

A three-star general flew in and talked privately with Cutter for more than an hour. Then an aide caught up with Barry and asked him if he would speak with the general.

Barry guessed the man to be close to sixty years old, with a chest filled with ribbons, and probably that many more in a drawer at home. He was very competent-looking.

He waved Barry to a seat and poured them both coffee. Cutter sat at the end of the long table. The general stared at Barry.

"We've wondered for a year if the rumors were true, Barry," the general said, stirring his sugared and creamed coffee. "And frankly, we hoped the rumors were valid. It will be my pleasure to report to . . . a very few people, in all branches of service, that I have met the Dog."

"Thank you, General."

"Orders are being cut this minute that will enable you and Cutter to duck into any Air Force base in the country for rest, repairs, equipment, whatever. At any time. Your rig is being loaded now with junk parts, the crates sealed and government stamped. Several of the crates—Cutter knows which ones—are filled with whatever you'll need to put a dent into the terrorist activities now building in America." He smiled. "And I mean . . . *whatever.*"

"Is this operation putting Cutter's career on the line?"

"No. Not at all. Technically, she's being reassigned to a top-secret unit working with certain groups in Europe. And she will be seen boarding a plane on this base. Her orders will be handled by personnel on this very base. A look-alike will be seen getting off the plane in Europe. In reality, you'll pick her up at Reese AFB outside of Lubbock. Any questions so far?"

Barry shook his head.

"You know how to ride a motorcycle, Barry?"

"Sure."

"There'll be a couple of Harleys amid all the crates." The general smiled. "Who knows, they might come in handy getting in and out of places your rig can't go."

Barry returned the smile.

"That Husky of yours bites."

"Yeah, I know. Did he get you, General?"

"Came damn close. I made the mistake of opening the door to your truck. Thing came at me like a black and white devil. I like to shit!"

Both Barry and Cutter laughed at the expression on the general's face.

The general laughed with them and stood up, holding out his hand to Barry. "Luck to you, Dog."

"Thank you, General."

He turned to Cutter. Held out his hand. Silver bars. He flipped them to her. "Congratulations, Captain Cutter. And good hunting." He smiled. "That's unofficial, of course."

He walked out the door without looking back.

Barry noted the stunned expression on Cutter's face. "I gather the promotion was not expected?"

"Damn sure wasn't." She slipped the bars into a pocket of her jacket. "Promotions are extremely difficult to come by in this unit."

"Sort of like an A-team, I would imagine."

She studied him. "I felt that you had been a part of some special force."

"Long time ago. Of course, Cutter, this just might mean something else for you."

"What?"

"When our run is over, you'll probably be given your own special operations teams."

"I hadn't thought of that." She smiled. "That would be a first."

"And you owe it all to women's lib," Barry said with a smile.

"Screw women's lib!" Cutter told him. "I got where I am by hard work, not by bitching and bra-burning."

"Anytime you want to burn your bra, let me know. I'll be happy to take it off for you."

"I'll hold you to that."

"Delighted."

"Let's go check out the gear the general arranged for us."

Together, they laid it out on the ground. And it was impressive. Rocket launchers, grenades, two M-60 machine guns, crates of ammunition, C-3 and C-4 with all sorts of detonators, including radio-controlled dets. Two thick rolls of det cord, and several crates of backup equipment. The general had thought of it all, and provided it for them.

They carefully repacked and stored it, then went back to the guarded compound.

Frenchy and Ready, Smooth and Mustard were waiting by their rumbling rigs.

"We got orders, Barry," Frenchy said. "We're gettin' ready to pull out soon as our escorts get here."

Barry shook his hand. "Been good runnin' with you boys."

"Same here. You and Cutter take it easy. We see you on the slab, we'll give you a bump."

"We'll keep our eyes open for you."

Handshakes were offered all around and taken. Cutter and Barry walked away.

Dog was jumping up and down, playing with a female security officer he had taken up with.

Barry knelt down beside the Husky and petted him. "You're

going to be in good hands, Dog. And a hell of a lot safer here. I'll see you in a few weeks."

Dog licked Barry's face and then went running off with the security officer.

"Acts like he's used to this," Cutter observed.

"He is. We're going to be moving fast and dangerous for a while. I feel better knowing Dog is safe. Besides," Barry grinned, "Dog is no fool. He always takes up with some good-looking woman."

Barry watched as Cutter's plane took off. He turned and went back to his rig. It had been checked from front bumper to tail. He inspected the hidden compartments in the custom-built cab and sleeper. Filled to capacity with an assortment of weapons and explosives.

Breaking dawn.

Barry looked around him. He was alone in the compound and knew that was deliberate. If you didn't see anything, you couldn't talk about it later.

He stood by the rumbling rig for a moment, then climbed up into the cab and checked his gauges. The big custom-built Cummins was as smooth as honey.

He turned on his bank of radios and dropped the rig into gear.

The engine growled.

The Dog was on the hunt.

He was waved through the back gate at Reese AFB without even a check and a security vehicle pulled in front of him and escorted him to a back runway. The brakes were still hissing when Cutter climbed on board. Her clothing was already in the sleeper.

They rolled out, following the security Jeep. Within a few

minutes, they were clear of the base and rolling toward highway 385.

"Orders?" Barry said.

"The government has leaked that we're carrying Stinger missiles to the west coast. Stay on three-eighty-five until we hit Interstate forty." She reached around and opened a bag, taking out an Uzi and laying it on the floor. "Then get ready for all hell to break loose."

They connected with 385 at Levelland and Barry pointed the nose of the Kenworth north. Interstate 40 lay some one hundred and fifteen miles north.

Cutter shifted her shapely butt and looked at Barry. "I've been in constant briefings since landing, Barry. All indications point to Darin Grady having linked up with Khaled. Khaled's people have linked up with the Islamic Army, this particular branch headed by a wacko from Chicago who now calls himself Bakhitar. He changed his name when he supposedly converted to the Moslem religion. This Bakhitar may be a fool, but he's got several hundred hard-core followers. And they need weapons. All of the terrorist groups are in constant need of weapons."

"Let me guess why: they're growing."

"Right. The real brains behind the American Islamic Army is someone known only to us as Ja. Ja supposedly lives somewhere in Central California and has twenty or thirty or more real hard professionals always on call."

"Do the powers that be in the House and Senate know of this growing threat of terrorism?"

"Maybe some of them. But if they ever do decide to get off their rumps and do something, they'll first have to have twelve months of public hearings and then reach the conclusion that it's okay to fight terrorism, but only if we don't use violence."

Barry laughed at the expression on her face and the heat in her voice. "That's why I'm here, Cutter. That's why the rules were bent and broken to put me here. But I agree with you. One hundred percent."

"There is one other thing, Barry. Well, more than one, of

course, but I think you'd better know that a rather generally disliked reporter for a national news organization, organization being spelled T-V, has been in contact with a known agent for I-7 and several other terrorist groups. Darin Grady has agreed to meet with this reporter for a sum of money. You want to take it from there?"

"This reporter hates the military, hates the cops, hates the government, et cetera, but professes to do what he is doing for the good of the country."

"I'm glad to see we're on the same wavelength."

"And this reporter would just love to learn about someone like me."

"Bingo."

"Well, then, we have two choices, Cutter."

She waited.

"We either get to Grady before he talks to this reporter, or we get to the reporter."

"You mean *kill* him!"

"I would rather it didn't come to that. I'd like to think the man could be convinced to lay off the story."

"Are you serious? That man would toss his own mother into a tub full of piranha for a story like this. People like that don't really care about the country, Barry. To profess to be so worldly, they are some of the most naive people I have ever encountered. They seem to want a perfect world but don't have sense enough to realize that's impossible." She paused. "And why are you grinning like that?"

"I just wanted to see how close our philosophies were. Pretty damned close, Cutter."

She shook her head. "Killing a big-name reporter, Barry. I don't know about that."

Barry laughed.

"You see something amusing about all this, Dog?"

"I really do, Cutter. Get on the radio and tell Reese we've had a change of plans. That reporter lives in Washington, doesn't he?"

"Yeah. So?"

"Tell control at Reese we'll be heading east instead of west."

"Barry! . . ."

"If we push hard, we can make it in thirty hours."

"Jesus Christ, Barry! You kill a nationally known reporter and all hell is going to break loose!"

"You're hurting my feelings, Cutter. Did I say anything about killing anybody?"

"Well, what the hell are we going to Washington for?"

" 'For' is a preposition, isn't it?"

"Of course it is. What the hell has that got to do with killing someone?"

"Nothing."

"Barry! . . ."

"I was always taught that one should not end a sentence with a preposition."

Cutter folded her arms under her breasts and cussed. Not cursed. Cussed. Old fashion swearing. Lots of four-letter words.

"Are you quite through, Cutter?"

She wasn't.

Barry waited.

"Now I'm through," she announced.

"I can just see Jackson's face and hear him," Barry said with a chuckle.

"You want to let me in on the joke?"

"He's going to go right through the roof."

"How fast are we going, Barry?"

"Sixty. Why?"

"If I balled this hand into a fist." She showed him. "And hit you on the jaw, what do you think would happen?"

"I think we'd probably have a wreck. Why do you ask?"

"Because if you don't tell me what you're planning on doing, I'm going to knock the crap flat out of you!"

He told her.

She started laughing. "You're right," she finally said, wiping her eyes. "Jackson is going to go right through the ceiling."

9

George Stanton stepped out of his bachelor apartment that overlooked the Potomac and walked to the elevator. He stepped in and his eyes immediately took in the luscious-looking lady standing by the rather hard-looking man with the cold dark eyes.

He smiled at the lady.

She returned the smile.

The man spoke very pleasantly to George. George returned the salutation. First appearances can be so deceiving, he thought. Fellow probably had an impoverished childhood. But worked his way out of it to become a success. George knew a tailor-made suit when he saw one.

"I love your special reports, Mr. Stanton," the lovely lady said. "I particularly enjoy your stand on handguns and all that horrible violence in the streets of this country."

"Thank you." Did the lady wink at him? She sure did. Well, she obviously knew quality when she saw it.

"I simply abhor violence," the man lisped.

Ye Gods! George thought. The man was a fag!

The lady smiled at him. Licked her lips.

No doubt about it, George thought, this lovely thing was coming on to him.

The elevator stopped. George certainly didn't want this momentous encounter to end. Good. They were walking toward the front. Time for a few more words. If he could shake that fruit the evening would be memorable.

"I have a car coming for me," George said, consulting his watch. "Should be here at any moment. Can I give you both a lift?"

The lady stepped closer. She smelled wonderful. But the handgun she stuck in his gut was something less than wonderful.

He could not believe his ears when the elegant lady said, "You can yell. But one second after you do, I'm going to blow your guts around your backbone if you have one!"

"What do you want?" George managed to croak. George was not a coward. But he was no fool, either. The lovely lady had managed to change like a chameleon. Her eyes were just as hard as the man's. And George knew, with a sinking feeling, the man was no pansy.

"Walk with us," the man said. "You stay in the middle. Your car shows up, you tell the driver you're having dinner with us. Keep walking. That's good. Do as you're told, you won't get hurt."

"I'm being kidnapped."

"For ten or fifteen thousand miles, yeah," the man told him. George thought about that. "What?"

"You'll see. We're turning here."

They walked toward a car. Stopped. The man unlocked the car and shoved George into the front seat. The woman got under the wheel, the man in the backseat.

"Make one little bobble, Stanton, and you're dead."

"I don't want to die."

"Then you won't. Just do as you're told and I'll guarantee you a news story that will top anything you've ever done."

George, with a reporter's intuition, began sensing that if he cooperated, he would not be harmed. And, also with a reporter's intuition, he sensed he was sitting on top of a story that would put him right up there on top of the heap.

He said nothing as Cutter slid easily into the traffic flow and turned toward Roosevelt Bride, heading into Virginia.

They were in Virginia before Barry said, "We'll get clear and then I'll call."

"Should be interesting. Leave the car at the motel?"

"Yes. It's been arranged."

"Who are you going to call?" Stanton asked.

"Santa Claus," Cutter told him.

Stanton folded his arms across his chest and stared out the windshield.

"What size jeans and shirt and boots do you wear, reporter?" Barry spoke. "I already know your hat size. They don't make a hat to fit your swelled head."

Stanton bit back a sharp retort and gave his clothing sizes.

"We'll get you outfitted along the way. Cutter, pull over into that service station and get Mr. Stanton a soft drink."

"I don't believe I care for anything, thank you."

"Shut up."

Once more rolling, Stanton looked at the strawberry soda in disgust. "I would have preferred a diet drink."

Barry held out his hand, over the backseat. Several pills in his palm.

Stanton looked at the pills. "I absolutely, positively refuse to take those things."

"It'll take me a little while, but I can arrange to get a suppository," Barry told him.

"And a stick to shove them where the sun don't shine," Cutter added.

Stanton took the pills without any further discussion. "I suppose you've drugged me?"

"That is correct. You'll be sound asleep in about thirty minutes."

"The network will not deal with kidnappers. You won't get a penny out of them."

"I wouldn't pay a penny for you either, Stanton," Barry said. "Relax. We're not after money."

"Then what do you want?"

"Certainly not your body," Cutter informed him.

She pulled into a motel and parked by a truck. "You change," Barry said. "I'll watch him."

She was back in a few minutes, dressed in blue jeans, leather jacket, and boots. She got in the backseat, a pistol in her hand, and Barry went into the motel room.

"That's an automatic pistol, isn't it?" Stanton asked.

"It's an auto-*loader,* Stanton. I wish you guardians of the truth would get things straight. I once listened to one of your kind moan about somebody getting shot with an automatic revolver. In all fairness, someone did invent one, about a hundred years ago. It didn't catch on."

"I stand corrected. We can't know everything, miss."

"What you people don't know would fill volumes."

Stanton yawned. "Excuse me."

"Quite all right."

"What gauge weapon is that thing?"

Cutter sighed and shook her head. "Shotguns have gauges, Stanton. Rifles and pistols have calibers. Some are even referred to in millimeters. This is a three-eighty."

"Who are you people?"

"You're going to find out, Stanton. Believe me." She watched the motel room door open and Barry point toward the truck.

"Out, Stanton. Walk toward the rig."

"The what?"

"The truck. Move."

She prodded him quickly across the blacktop, the muzzle of the .380 quickening his step. Barry had opened the door.

"Climb up and get in the sleeper."

It took him a couple of tries to make it, but he finally got into the truck. He banged his shin a couple of times and managed to fall into the bunk.

"Take off your shoes and jacket," Cutter told him. "Loosen your tie. You're about to go beddy-bye."

"Your humor is grotesque!"

"Just relax, Stanton. Like the proctologist said: you might enjoy it."

Barry laughed.

Stanton did not see the humor in it. He lay back and could not stop a huge yawn.

"Won't be long now," Barry's voice came to him in a hollow fog. "You ready to roll?"

"Anytime."

The last thing Stanton remembered was Cutter covering him with a blanket and the rumble of the truck as it rolled away from the city.

"Where in the hell have you been? Goddammit, Dog!" Jackson yelled. "You've been out of contact for a day and a half."

Barry told him.

Jackson was silent for a moment. Heavy breathing. Then he shrieked, "Kidnap George Stanton! Holy jumping Jesus Christ, Dog! You can't kidnap a nationally known reporter!"

"Oh, yeah! We just did. He's in the truck. Sound asleep."

"You've lost your goddamn mind. Minds. Both of you!"

"Settle down, Jackson. Call the networks. Anonymously. Advise them that Stanton is all right. No harm will come to him. Tell them it would be best if they make no mention of Stanton's disappearance . . ."

"Barry! . . ."

"Shut up, Jackson. Tell them that when Stanton is released, he'll have the biggest story of this decade. Tell them they'll be receiving a tape of Stanton in about a day."

"Barry! . . ."

"You got all that, Jackson?"

"Goddammit, Barry. You . . ."

Barry hung up.

Back on the road, heading west, Cutter said, "How did Jackson take the news?"

"Predictably. Now we'll see how the network reacts. We'll stop at the first truck stop and get some clothes for Stanton and pick up a tape recorder. I want Stanton to record a message and we'll send it air express to the network. I'll call them first thing in the morning and advise them it's on the way. There's an air mattress in the storage area. We can sleep on the floor. Got to keep our guest happy, you know?"

Stanton slept for eight hours and Barry and Cutter each caught enough sleep to keep them going. Stanton woke about an hour before dawn. He was confused and totally disoriented. With a groan, he pushed back the blanket and sat up. He lay back down with a moan after banging his head on a shelf. It was cushion-leather padded and it was more a shock than painful.

"Where in God's name am I?" he croaked.

"Charleston, West Virginia," Cutter told him. She poured him coffee from a freshly filled thermos and he took it gratefully.

"Thank you," he said, after a sip. "I must say, for kidnappers, you're treating me quite nicely."

"We're not your ordinary kidnappers, George," Barry told him. "We grabbed you for educational purposes, not for ransom."

"Educational purposes? Whose?"

"Yours." Cutter twisted in the seat, looking at him. She handed him a sack. "Bacon and egg sandwiches in there. We just got them so they're still warm."

"Thank you. I am quite hungry." His feet touched a large sack on the floor of the sleeper.

"Your new clothes, George," Barry said, without turning around. He had heard the sack rustle.

"Where do I change?"

"Just lower the leather flap for privacy," Cutter told him. "And in case you're thinking about the door to the sleeper . . .

forget it." She pointed to a bank of key-lock switches on the huge dash. "Electronically locked."

"This is no ordinary truck," George accurately guessed. "This compartment I'm in was custom-built and really quite comfortable."

"That's correct, George. The taxpayers' money was well-spent, don't you think?"

"I don't understand. Taxpayers' money?"

"You're in a one-of-a-kind truck, George. Technically, it's called an SST. Safe Secure Transport. But most are not this fancy."

Cutter picked it up. "SSTs haul weapons and nuclear parts across the country. They are not pyrophoric, not primed, and not integral."

"In English, they won't blow up." George spoke around a mouthful of sandwich.

"That is correct."

"That is so comforting to know," George said drily.

Both Barry and Cutter laughed. Cutter said, "George, you'd probably be a nice guy if you weren't such a pompous jerk."

"Was that supposed to be a compliment?"

"In a way."

George left the bed and sat on the floor to better hear. His eyes found the Uzi lying on the floor by Cutter's feet. "I know what that is. I did my bit in Lebanon."

"If you're thinking of grabbing it," Barry warned him, "I can assure you, you'll be dead before your hand reaches it."

"I have never fired a weapon in my life. I have no intention of starting now."

"You were never in the Army?"

"No. Thank God."

They rode in silence for a few miles. The sky was graying behind them, shooting up silver rays.

Cutter and Barry had agreed to level as much as possible with the reporter. But he was going to have to ask the questions.

George drank his coffee and held out the cup, Cutter refilling it. "You both work for the government, don't you?"

"That is correct, George. All SST drivers work for the government."

George smiled. "I have this suspicion that you both are much more than mere truck drivers. Both of you have the bearing of military people."

"One of us is," Cutter told him, leaving him to guess which one.

He didn't pick up on it. The lights of Charleston faded behind as they rolled on westward, at a steady 65 mph.

"What do you people do, besides drive a truck?"

"We fight terrorism, George," Barry told him. He crossed the river, picking up Interstate 64, heading for Huntington.

"I . . . see. Legally?"

"Depends on your interpretation of legal."

"You're being as honest as you think you can be with me. I appreciate that. But I still don't know why you kidnapped me or what you want."

"We know that you had planned on meeting with Darin Grady," Cutter told him.

"Did you now?" George said softly, his voice just audible over the truck noise. "That is interesting."

"What is interesting to us is why you would even want to interview the son of a bitch," Barry said. "Most of you people claim to hate guns, yet you'll give a murderous terrorist a lot of air time. That doesn't make a lot of sense to me."

"The man is fighting for a free Ireland."

"Horseshit!" Cutter spat it out. "Would you give the Bader-Meinhof gang as much time? How about the Aryan Nations? The Islamic Army? Did you know they are all connected? One helps the other and have been doing so for a couple of decades."

"Can you prove that?"

"Yes."

"I'd like to see that proof."

"You will. I promise you that."

"You will forgive me if I don't place a great deal of credence in your word."

"Perfectly understandable, George," Barry said.

"You need to go to the bathroom?" Cutter asked.

"Yes."

"Rest area just up ahead." Barry made up his mind. "George, we're bait. Pure and simple. We lure terrorists out to strike at us, and then we neutralize them."

George laughed, and surprisingly enough to both of them, there was good humor in the laughter. Amazing how the man could be such a horse's ass on the TV and fairly likeable in person.

"By neutralize, you mean kill them."

"That is correct."

"Then what Darin's spokesperson said was not fantasy. I wondered about that."

"I don't know. What was said?"

"That the government of the United States had killers in its employ."

"George, until all governments stop having killers on their payrolls, and all do, all other governments must do likewise."

"We can certainly argue that."

"And probably will."

"You're offering me quite a story."

"Yes."

"Why didn't you just come to me with it?" Then he paused and laughed. "Foolish question, wasn't it?"

"Yes."

George was silent for a moment. "Amazing. I'm in the presence of killers, yet I don't feel even a touch of fear."

"We're not going to hurt you, George."

"You're taking me on a mission, aren't you?"

"Yes." Barry swung into the rest area and parked. He twisted in the seat and looked at George.

George scratched his chin. "We have an affiliate in Louisville. I'd like to stop and pick up a mini-cam. On the way, I'll call my network and tell them I'm here voluntarily. I would assume some . . . spokesperson from the government has already called."

"That is correct. The mini-cam is all right. But you can't take pictures of this truck, or of us."

"Agreed."

"Bathroom is that way, George," Cutter said, pointing and opening the door.

"You realize, of course, that I'm going to blow your operation clear out of the water?"

"I don't think you will." Barry leveled with him. "I think when you see that terrorism must be fought on the same level as the terrorists, you'll report it fairly."

"You're taking a terrible chance."

"Maybe."

"Truthfully, did you consider killing me when you heard I was going to meet with Darin?"

"Yes."

George blinked. Paled just a bit. "The news media is hated that much among certain people?"

"Yes."

"But we report the truth!"

"As you see it."

"Perhaps. The camera doesn't lie."

Both Barry and Cutter laughed at that.

George allowed himself a small smile. "I'm free to go to the restroom alone?"

"Certainly."

"Suppose I run?"

"I'll find you," Barry told him.

George got the message. And the message reminded him how desperately he needed to pee.

10

Barry and Cutter hadn't taken much of a chance letting George go to the restroom alone. There were no phones in the restroom and the outside pay phone was in plain view. Both Barry and Cutter felt they could outrun the reporter if he decided to bolt.

They had taken his pens from his jacket as he slept, so he couldn't leave a note.

Any fears they might have felt, however slight, proved groundless. George Stanton was back in the truck within five minutes. He dropped the leather flap and changed clothes while the rig was being eased out of the parking lot and back onto the interstate.

"First time I've had on jeans in years," he was heard to mutter.

He raised the flap and accepted another cup of coffee, sitting on the floor.

"You said you were bait. When does the fishing start."

"Anytime," Cutter told him, behind the wheel. "You're sitting on enough firepower to start a small revolution."

Stanton looked confused.

"Sit on the bunk," Barry told him, sliding from his passenger seat. He pulled up the Velcro-held section of carpet and lifted the hinged door.

Stanton sat and stared at the arsenal. He pointed to a small bag.

"Grenades," Barry said. He touched a box. "Filled clips for Uzis and M-16s." He touched a padded section. "Two sawed-off pump riot guns and a Remington seven-millimeter magnum rifle with scope. For long-range work."

"Sniper rifle," the reporter said.

"That is correct."

Stanton pointed. "That?"

"C-three and C-four. Plastic explosives. Detonators over here."

Barry closed the lid and smoothed down the carpet. The compartment was perfectly covered.

"How many trucks like this does the government have on the road?"

"Equipped like we are?"

"Yes."

"Just this one. I told you: it's a one-of-a-kind truck."

"The paranoia over terrorism in the United States has reached this level then?" He sat back down on the floor and patted the hidden compartment.

"It isn't paranoia, George. Much of what's happening in the U.S. just isn't reported."

"Are you once again blaming the media for that?"

"No. Many acts of terrorism, after or before the fact, aren't made public."

"The government is deliberately withholding vital information from the public!" George sounded a tad huffy about that.

"For a good reason, George," Cutter told him.

"There is never a good reason for that."

Barry and Cutter smiled at each other, Cutter saying, "We simply don't want the press to piss and moan and distort the facts about how we deal with terrorists."

Stanton stared at her. "But we don't do that!"

"Do you really believe that?" Barry asked him.

"Well, of course, I believe it!"

"We'll try to show you where you're wrong," Cutter said.

"I know what you're saying." The reporter met the gaze of

Barry. "You people, the hard right-wingers, want the national press to become your pawns. To report what you want us to report."

"That isn't true," Cutter said. "What we would like is for the press to report both sides of any chosen issue and to understand that many of the problems facing this nation cannot be dealt with in a strictly constitutional manner. When you fight terrorism, you first have to understand it, to begin to think like a terrorist, and then fight them on their own level . . . but do it better."

George had not taken his eyes from the woman. Which was no task at all. "You're the military person here, aren't you?"

"Yes."

"Are there many like you?"

"Not nearly enough."

"Have you killed terrorists, miss?"

"Yes. Eight or nine, I'm not sure of the count."

"You say that with about as much emotion as ordering a hamburger. You're taking a human life."

"Human life is the cheapest commodity on the face of the earth, George." Barry startled him. "Ask any terrorist. We're down in the trenches now. With the rats and the snakes and the slime."

"And you, both of you, are slime-free?"

"No," Cutter admitted. "Unfortunately, no. That's what you and your colleagues can't understand. Or won't understand. The constitutional rights, civil rights, and many of the other so-called guarantees have been stretched to the breaking point. All you people can do is bemoan the rights of the poor criminal."

George didn't like that, and it showed on his face. But he was smart enough to know he was up against a stone wall with Barry and Cutter.

He crawled back into the bunk and stretched out. "Wake me up when we get to Louisville, please."

* * *

George Stanton called his network from the Louisville affiliate. He told them he'd had a chance to get a toehold on what just might be the biggest story of the decade and had to leave in a hurry.

He didn't know anything about any kidnapping or any phone call from some man. It was probably a crank call. Disregard it.

The network told George that they would agree only if a cameraman be allowed to accompany him; that would insure that his story about being safe was true.

"Four people in the truck?" Cutter said to Barry. "No way!"

Barry put in a call to Jackson from the motel in Louisville.

"I wouldn't trust that damned Stanton any further than I could toss an elephant," Jackson said.

"Oddly enough," Barry said. "I do trust him. And if he gets this story right, it could mean a real step forward in combatting terrorism."

"It could also mean the end of your work," Jackson reminded the Dog. "Not to mention hurting the administration very badly."

"I'm aware of that. But I think it's a risk worth taking to **get** some press types on our side, instead of them taking cheap shots at anyone trying to get the government back to dead center."

"It's your ass, Dog. Your show."

Jackson hung up.

Barry called the Louisville station. Stanton had taken a cab from the motel.

"Call your cameraman, George. Tell your network people that there might be days at a stretch where you'll be out of touch. I'll get busy arranging transportation for you."

While George was arranging for a cameraman, Cutter was on the horn to her people, setting up a vehicle.

"The cameraman will be here on the four-fifteen flight from National," George informed them.

"You'll be driving a Ford Bronco," Barry told him. "You'll

be handed the keys at the airport. Don't ask the person any questions. Just stow your gear and move out."

"Real cloak-and-dagger stuff, huh, Barry?"

Barry ignored that. "The Bronco will be fully radio-equipped. Preset and turned on. Get on Interstate sixty-four and stay on it. We'll pick you up."

"Where?"

"We'll pick you up, George. Don't sweat it. See you some-time tonight."

Barry hung up. Turned to Cutter. "Let's get the hell out of here."

Cutter and Barry were waiting in a rest area in Illinois when the Bronco rolled past. It had been dark for several hours.

Barry rolled out onto the slab and caught up with the Bronco. He lifted the mike to his lips. "Heads up, George. We're sitting on your donkey."

"My what?" George radioed back.

Cutter took the mike. "Your ass."

Several seconds of silence on the scrambled frequency. "Oh. Yes, I see. Now what?"

"That doesn't look like a cameraman, George."

"It isn't. Her name is Bonnie. She's one of the best."

"I'll take your word for that. Last name?"

"O'Neal."

Cutter and Barry exchanged glances.

"Wonderful," Cutter muttered.

"Lots of Americans are named O'Neal and O'Brian and O'Mally and O'-whatever, Cutter. Ninety-nine percent of them would spit on a terrorist if they saw one."

"And that other one percent?"

"I know what you mean."

"Are you there?" George radioed.

"Can't you see us?"

"That's not what I meant!"

"We'll pull ahead of you people," Barry told him. "Stay with us. We'll pick up seventy in St. Louis and take that most of the way west. These radios will knock your hat off for a hundred miles or more. It's doubtful we'll lose contact. Are either of you hungry?"

Both were.

"Trucking with these two just might turn out to be a real pain in the butt," Cutter bitched.

Barry laughed at her, then keyed the mike. "We'll eat in St. Louis. I'm coming around you now. Stay with me and don't worry about the speed limit."

Barry signaled, pulled over into the left lane, and came around the Bronco. Both of them caught a glimpse of a short blonde sitting on the passenger side.

"Looks cute." Barry stuck the needle to Cutter.

She rolled her eyes and chose not to reply.

"I'm Barry and this is Cutter." He introduced them to Bonnie O'Neal.

Where Cutter was tall and shapely and dark-haired and lovely, Bonnie was short and shapely and blonde and lovely. Fair-skinned and blue-eyed. She looked like she could take care of herself, and probably had on more than one occasion.

Barry had been around the horn himself a time or two and could tell when interest sprang into a woman's eyes. And with Bonnie, it didn't just spring, it came snarling and hissing.

"Just Barry and Cutter?" Bonnie asked.

"They'll do," Barry told her. "You two go on and get something to eat." He handed George a large thermos. "When you come back, have this filled with coffee, black, and a sack full of sandwiches."

"You're not joining us?" George asked.

"We can't leave the rig. Too easy for someone to slap explosives on us."

"Isn't that being a bit melodramatic?" Bonnie asked.

"Understand this now," Cutter said, a touch of heat in her tone. "I've had twenty-five thousand dollars on my head for the last two years. Most of the people I work with have rewards out on them from various terrorist groups. Barry tops the list. He's got a hundred and fifty thousand dollars on his head. They would prefer to catch us alive, so they could torture us. I've personally seen what they did to one woman." Her eyes locked into Bonnie's blues. "Imagine the most horrible of perversions, and then magnify it a hundred times. And what they can do to male agents is equally awful. Melodramatic, Miss O'Neal? No. Now, do you understand all that?"

"Perfectly. Oh, and Cutter. My grandparents were killed in an IRA ambush about five years ago. I have two cousins in the S.A.S. I just thought you'd like to know. And here's something else for you to chew on: Big tall chicks who think they're tough don't impress me worth a fuck!"

She spun around and walked off.

George cleared his throat. "I didn't have time to warn either of you. Bonnie can be extremely crude at times. Well, I'll get you something to eat and some coffee. See you in a few minutes."

Barry chuckled. "This run should be quite interesting, Cutter."

Cutter turned slowly and stared at him. "Dog, screw you!"

"Think we have time before they return?"

She socked him on the arm. Left a bruise that stayed with him for a week.

11

Dawn found them a few miles west of Topeka, Kansas, Cutter driving. She was just signaling for a turn into a rest area when Barry climbed out of the bunk and slipped into the seat.

"Trouble?" he asked.

"No. But I imagine that's a pretty tired pair back there, don't you?"

"I'm sure. It's about ten hours from here to Denver, and I want us all to be heads-up fresh. If it's all right with you, we'll run until about noon and check into a motel. Let them shower and rest for a few hours in a bed. We'll take turns watching the truck. Okay?"

"Sounds good to me."

While Cutter went to the bathroom, Barry walked back to the Bronco.

"We'll run for a few more hours, then pull over and get some motel rooms. You both can shower and get some rest in a bed."

"And you and Cutter?" George asked.

"We'll rent a room, but only one of us will be in it at a time. The truck has to be guarded."

"Barry?" Bonnie got out of the Bronco. "I'm sorry I popped off to Cutter back up the road. Perhaps it's partly because both of you seem to take this job so seriously and because George has told me how you both feel about the press."

"We take it seriously, Bonnie, because both our asses are

on the line. I'm sure as a cameraperson you've been under fire."

She nodded her head.

"Not a very enjoyable experience, was it?"

"No."

"Fine. Then you'll understand why we appear so ready at all times."

Her face tightened at that.

"George told you our deal about the film and the copy?"

"Yes."

"And you don't like it?"

"Not worth a damn!"

"Well, Bonnie. It's like my mother used to say about castor oil: you might not like it, but it's good for you."

"I don't understand the comparison."

"Because if you try to sneak film past me, even if you do succeed in airing it, I'll kill you."

Barry turned and walked away.

Bonnie looked at George. "Do you believe him?"

"Oh, yes. You remember the stories we've heard about that combination Robin Hood/vigilante truck driver that's been roaming the highways for about a year?"

"Sure. Just stories, that's all."

George shook his head. "All true. I just put it together. You just met the Dog, my dear."

They checked into a motel at Hays, Kansas. Barry offered to stay with the truck the first shift, allowing Cutter to take a long bath and some sleep in a king-size bed. He didn't get any argument from her about that.

They had made the run in just over four hours and Barry was going to let them all rest a full eight hours. He planned to be back on the road by about nine that night.

He felt they would be hit that night; and the logical spot

would be in Colorado, between Limon and Byers, on that stretch of Interstate 70 that turned and ran northwest.

Barry had showered and shaved and changed into fresh clothing. He told Cutter he'd see her in about five or six hours.

He was making a visual inspection of the truck when he sensed movement behind him. He spun around, the 9mm in his hand.

Bonnie.

"Whoa!" she held up a hand, her face paling just a bit. "Damn, you people are jumpy, aren't you?"

"We manage to stay alive." He tucked the 9mm back into a shoulder rig, then checked his watch. "You didn't get much sleep, Bonnie."

"Four hours. That's about all I ever get or need."

"Let's get in the truck. It's cold out here."

She climbed up and sat in the passenger seat, looking very much like a school kid. A well-endowed school kid.

"You can sure see a lot from up here, can't you?"

Barry said nothing. Just wondered what she wanted. He wasn't sure he trusted her.

She cut her blues at him. "Are you the man that's called the Dog?"

"Where'd you hear that?"

"Talk. Gossip. Rumors."

Barry chose not to reply.

"You don't trust me, do you?"

"I don't trust any reporter or anyone who works for a news-gathering organization. Print or broadcast."

"You're trusting George."

"George is scared of me. With good reason. He knows if he lies to me or tries to pull some sneak-preview of films or copy that I haven't approved of, I'll kill him."

"I didn't believe you when you told me that a few hours ago."

"And now?"

"I guess I believe it. It's so preposterous it has a ring of truth to it."

"Don't guess, Bonnie. Just believe it."

"I'd like to hear the story of your life, Barry."

"Why?"

She smiled and shook her head. Barry liked the set of her chin and her mouth. She reminded him of another lady who used to be a reporter for a big network. He hadn't seen her for a long time; wondered what happened to her.

She caught him looking at her. "What are you thinking?"

"That I haven't been with a woman, sexually, for a long time."

"Cutter? You mean you haven't been sleeping with that big chick?"

"No. It isn't wise to mix business with pleasure."

"This is insane! I'm talking sex with a man I don't even know!"

"And don't even like," Barry added for her.

"I don't know about that. Maybe. You're . . . different. I hate these macho sons of bitches. They're the most superficial bunch of jock-bastards going. And most of them are stupid. What kind of music do you like?"

"I listen to all kinds. But I prefer, when I'm alone or relaxing, to listen to classical."

"No kidding? Me, too. Lots of bad stuff going around now."

Barry knew she wasn't talking about rock and roll music.

"Yeah, I know. The doctors say I'm not carrying nor contagious."

"It's all so complicated now," she said with a sigh. "I never did sleep around much. Only when the pressure got to the boiling point. Cold showers will work for just so long."

"I know that, too."

"That's hard to believe about you and Cutter."

"But true."

"She likes you, Barry. A lot. I can tell."

"She knows better than to let it go further."

"Why?"

"Because it would be an impossible situation. She knows it and I know it."

Dusk was spreading its gentle cloak around the land.

"Cutter will be out here any minute."

Bonnie cut her eyes toward him. "That's probably a lie. But whatever you say. You're not going to take your eyes off those mirrors long enough to make love, are you, Dog?"

"That's right . . . Bitch."

"In heat. You think I came out here to get you in that . . . thing back there"—she jerked a thumb toward the sleeper—"while someone plants a bomb on this truck, don't you?"

"That thought did enter my mind."

What he didn't tell her was that he had called Jackson and requested a fast security check on Miss Bonnie O'Neal. He was to pick it up in Denver.

Now he was going to set her up.

"You're a cold-blooded bastard, Dog."

He picked up a road map. "Even bastards get hard-ons, Bonnie."

"What the hell does a road map have to do with making out?"

"I'm just going to warn you. I figure on pulling out of here about nine o'clock. We'll be inside Colorado by that time. And that's when I figure they're going to hit us. Between the state line and Burlington. If we make it past that point, we can relax to Denver."

"George said you were running empty. Just junk. That you were only bait."

"I lied."

She knew better than to ask him what specifically he was pulling. For more than one reason. "I'll be in my room."

"You want me to scratch on the door or to just howl?"

She opened the door. "I don't know that I want you to do a goddamn thing." She stepped down the ladder and walked across the parking lot to her room.

Barry noted that she had a terrific ass.

* * *

Cutter slipped into the truck about forty-five minutes later. "You let me sleep too long. You should have awakened me."

"You needed the rest. Besides, I've been busy setting up Miss Bonnie."

"You sure you haven't been laying her down?"

"Not yet." He explained what he'd done and Cutter nodded her approval. "Have you eaten?"

"Yes. You go ahead and eat and nap for a while. Or screw Miss O'Neal. Whatever."

He grinned at her. "We all have to make sacrifices, Cutter. It's for the good of the country."

He left the truck in a hurry, before she could wind up and punch him again.

He ate and then walked to Bonnie's room. Pressing his ear to the door, he could hear her voice, but could not make out the words. He walked to George's room. Through a crack in the drapes, he could see the man sitting, watching TV. So Miss Bonnie must be on the phone.

But to whom?

He walked back to her room and listened. She was off the phone. He knocked softly on the door.

She opened it just a crack, peeking out at him. She stepped back and waved him on in. He noticed very quickly that she was not wearing a bra under her T-shirt.

"Where's the big chick?"

"In the truck."

"She won't leave it?"

"No."

She looked at her watch. "We've got two and a half hours before you said we'd pull out."

She was very defensive, her eyes cool.

All right, Barry thought. If that's the way you want to play it. "Yeah. Time for a short jump and a long nap."

She reared back and took a swing at him.

* * *

It hadn't been rape. Not exactly.

Barry's torn shirt lay in one corner of the room, Bonnie's equally ruined T-shirt in another corner. His cowboy boots were in a chair. Had she been able to put them where she at first told him she'd like to shove them, they would have needed a good polishing.

Her jeans were ruined, the zipper torn open. Barry's underwear shorts were ripped.

It had been mostly a silent struggle, and not one where either one of them had really been trying to hurt the other. It had been a power struggle.

Now she lay sleeping in his arms, both of them sexually satisfied. Barry had waited until her breathing had evened out into that sleep-rhythm that cannot be totally faked, and then he had silently fanned her luggage. A snub-nosed .38 and a half box of ammo. An address book. He memorized several of the names and numbers.

He replaced everything and slipped back into bed, gathering her into his arms.

Now he gently awakened her.

"Ummm."

"I've got to get back to my room and shower and change, Bonnie. Half hour to go before pullout."

"Let's don't talk about pullout. I haven't had one of those much talked about multiple things in a long, long time. For an old dude, you're pretty good."

"It's all the clean living I've done."

She called him a few uncomplimentary names and lay naked on the bed, watching him gather up his clothes.

"Anybody ever tell you you have nice buns?" Bonnie asked him.

"I can't say that they have."

Barry dressed as quickly as possible and got the hell back to his room.

"How was it?" Cutter asked.

"Cutter! . . ."

"Nice and tight?"

Barry sighed and decided to ride it out.

"She moved her ass a lot?"

Barry checked the gauges.

"She go down on you, Barry? Give you a good head-job?"

"When you are quite through, Cutter, we'll go over what I found in her room."

"That she isn't a natural blonde?"

"Oh, yeah. She's a natural blonde."

Cutter cussed him.

"Are you through?"

She wasn't.

When she wound down, Barry handed her a slip of paper. "Names and numbers I found in her address book. Have your people run them. I also found a thirty-eight and a half box of hollow-nosed ammo."

Cutter settled down to business. "A thirty-eight? That's odd for a network cameraperson, isn't it?"

"Maybe. They do go into some pretty hairy spots at times."

"Your choice of words, not mine."

"Cutter! . . ."

"Sorry. Couldn't resist one last stroke."

"Your choice of words, not mine."

She was still cussing him when they pulled out of the parking lot.

12

Cutter drove to near the state line, turning over the wheel to Barry at Goodland. Before taking the wheel, Barry walked back to the Bronco.

"Heads up, people." He looked at Bonnie, staring at him. "You tell George what I told you about the suspected ambush?"

She nodded her head.

"Got your camera all ready?"

Bonnie jerked a thumb toward the back. "Ready to go."

"Lay back a good mile. That ought to give you time to get out of the field of fire. See you."

Barry walked back to his rig and pulled out.

They rolled into Colorado and smoked past Burlington, heading west through the night. When they were halfway between the state line and Limon, Barry's speaker began talking to him.

"Looks like your hunch didn't prove out," Bonnie said.

"Bitch!" Cutter muttered.

Grinning, Barry picked up his mike. "Looks like it. Next stop is Denver."

"Ten-four."

"I hope Jackson managed to pick up some trash on that bitch," Cutter said darkly. She shook her head and smiled at

Barry. "I really don't, Barry. I'm just trying to keep up the game you started. But it did irritate me at first."

"Well, it was interesting for a time. Check the map and see if I'm right. If so, we should pick up a tail at one of four locations: forty and two-eighty-seven should be the first one. Then at seventy-one. Next one will be twenty-four, and the last one highway eighty-six."

"That's right. I'll opt for twenty-four. If so, they'll strike just past this last cutoff."

"That's the way I've got it figured. Check out the weapons, Cutter. Set them on full rock and roll and get ready to dance."

"Wish I knew who was driving back there," she pondered.

"Yeah. I'll keep my eyes open for some kind of signal. But even if she is up to her butt in slime, I don't think she'd tip her hand this early. If, and that's a big if, she's involved, she'll probably have been ordered to surface only as a last resort."

Cutter poured them coffee, handing Barry a cup. "I honestly hope Bonnie is level, Barry. Tell you the truth, I admire her brass in coming on to you."

"You're a professional, Cutter. You know why I haven't come on to you."

She smiled. "I can dream, can't I?"

"I guess that never hurts, Captain Cutter."

That had the desired effect: bringing to the fore why she was riding along in the middle of the night in a fortress of an 18-wheeler.

To fight terrorism.

She picked up her M-16, actually a shortened version of the weapon, called a CAR, and stared out the window into the darkness.

"I understand." Her words were softly offered, just audible over the rumbling.

"About ten miles to the first point," Barry said. "And I've been thinking about something: if there are terrorists lying in wait for us, they might try to take George. Have you considered that?"

"Are you a mind-reader, Barry? Yes. That's what I was thinking."

Barry picked up the mike. "George? Close up some." He watched the headlights close to about a half mile. "Stay alert, George. If anything goes down, take evasive action immediately and don't either of you try to be heroes. You understand?"

"Why are you telling us this now?" George radioed. "I thought the danger was past."

"The danger is always near, George. Call it a feeling in my guts."

"The camera won't pick up your stomach problems, Barry," Bonnie's voice came through the speaker. "You lied to us, didn't you?"

Cutter was watching him.

"Now why would I do that, Miss O'Neal."

"Because you don't trust me." Her words were flat.

"You got that right, honey," he muttered. He keyed the mike. "Now who's paranoid, Bonnie?"

No reply came through the speakers.

They rolled past the on-ramp of 40/287 with no one pulling in behind them.

"One down, three to go," Cutter said.

They passed 71 with the same results. The night was filled with gloom, the air smelling of rain. Traffic was practically non-existent. The lights of a big rig suddenly filled Barry's mirrors.

"Now where the hell did he come from?"

"He's closing fast, Dog!" Cutter spoke.

At the on-ramp of 24, two 18-wheelers suddenly pulled out of the darkness in front of them.

The rigs slowed to 50 mph.

"Get some armor-piercing ammo in that weapon, Cutter. I think you're going to have to shoot out some tires. Load up that big forty-four mag with Teflon-coat; the tires might throw off a two-twenty-three."

She quickly loaded up a Smith & Wesson model 29, six-inch barrel, and hooked two speed-loaders onto her belt.

"What's going on?" George asked.

"You're about to see some action, George. Heads up, people."

The 18-wheeler behind him roared around the Bronco and pulled in behind Barry. The 18-wheelers in front now controlled both lanes.

Barry and Cutter had been placed into a box.

"What the hell are those trucks doing?" George called.

"Trying to put us in a coffin, George," Cutter radioed back. "Stay off the radio unless you've got an emergency. We're going to be busy."

"Super-broad goes into action, huh?" Bonnie's voice filled the truck.

Barry smiled.

"I take back everything nice I might have thought about you, cunt!" Cutter muttered.

Barry laughed aloud.

The exit ramp of the last hole for many miles slid past. "Now the fun begins," Barry said.

He picked up his CB mike. "Get out of the way, you bastard!"

The 18-wheeler in the left lane flickered his running lights. But he made no attempt to speed up or fall back.

The rig behind Barry and Cutter was sitting smack on Barry's donkey.

Barry touched his brakes.

The driver behind him automatically did the same, but without losing any distance.

"He's a pro," Barry muttered, keying his CB mike. "Get off my tail, Driver!"

The rig behind him blinked his lights and stayed right on Barry's donkey.

Barry lowered his window and with his right hand, picked up his 9mm. "Hang on, Cutter."

He abruptly swung into the right lane, an instant later, standing on his brakes, driving one-handed, fighting to keep from losing the rig.

The driver behind him had no choice but to stay in the left lane. His tires were smoking, but still he passed Barry.

The man on the passenger side held what looked to Barry to be an MP5.

Barry's 9mm barked as fast as he could pull the trigger, the custom loads blowing fist-sized holes in the man's face, throat, and chest, the force of the exploding slugs slamming the man over and into the driver.

Barry stood on his brakes and watched as the rig slewed and then went over the side.

The two rigs in front of him roared on into the night, their lights fading and then vanishing into the darkness.

George pulled over on the shoulder, behind Barry, just as Barry and Cutter were climbing down.

Bonnie had her mini-cam on her shoulder, recording.

"They were trying to hijack you!" George shouted, his voice filled with excitement. "We saw it all and heard you ask them to let you past. How did the driver lose control, do you imagine?"

Barry looked at the reporter. Sighed. "Because I shot the hell out of them."

George blinked. "Gunfire?"

"Yeah, George. Gunfire. From one of those horrible handguns you're always moaning about. Come on. I want you to get this on film. And we don't have much time."

Barry led the way to the wrecked rig. The trailer had broken off and had gone rolling several hundred yards away. The tractor had rolled a couple of times and then landed on its wheels.

Nine-millimeter in hand, Barry jerked open the door on the passenger side and the body of the codriver fell out, half his face missing from the impacting of the exploding bullets.

Bonnie gasped and George got sick.

Barry climbed up and looked inside. Place was a mess. He

handed Cutter two MP5 submachine guns. She showed them to Bonnie and George. Bonnie was filming.

"Standard trucker equipment, right?" Cutter stuck the needle to George.

Bonnie's smile was tight, but she kept her mouth shut. George opened his mouth to speak, then realized anything he might say in defense of the dead men would be more than neutralized by the presence of the submachine guns.

Barry tossed a bag to the ground. "Open it and film it," he ordered.

The bag was filled with grenades. Bonnie filmed the deadly contents.

Barry climbed down after inspecting and jotting down the names and addresses of the dead men. "Gather up all this crap," he ordered. "We don't want this to look like anything other than an accident."

"But the men have bullet holes in them!" George protested.

Barry smiled and reached into his jacket pocket, pulling out an object.

Cutter laughed.

"What's that?" George demanded.

"Incendiary," Cutter told him. "Come on, you two. Let's get the hell out of here."

Barry backed up, pulled the pin, and tossed the grenade into the cab of the truck.

A ball of flame enveloped the tractor as Barry was running up the slope and crossing the highway. Cutter was already behind the wheel and slowly rolling as Barry climbed on board.

The flames from the burning tractor filled the night.

They faded from view as the two-vehicle convoy rounded a curve.

"They won't try again tonight, will they?" George radioed.

"They'll try," Barry told him. "So stay loose and be ready for anything."

"I bet they're not ten miles up the road," Cutter said.

"No bets, Cutter. We've tweaked the tail of the terrorists and they've declared war on us. They're going to pull out all the stops now."

She noticed he was smiling. "The Dog is on the prowl, huh?"

"You bet your sweet ass, Cutter."

"How would you know anything about *my* ass!"

13

If it's the last thing I ever do, Barry was thinking, I'm going to bed this woman down or she's never going to let up on me.

But his eyes had picked up on the familiar running lights of two 18-wheelers just ahead of him.

"I see them," he said, before Cutter could speak.

"There they are!" George's excited voice came through the speaker. "Let's call the police! I'll testify in any court of law about those two trucks."

Cutter cut her eyes to Barry. "How do people get so naive? You ever thought about that, Barry?"

"I think they have to work on it. Real hard."

"Are you going to answer me!" George yelled.

Barry lifted the mike to his lips. "George, we're not here to see that these people get their constitutional due. They're terrorists. You see how they're stopping to call the cops, don't you? They're so overcome with respect for our judicial system they just can't wait to get to the nearest phone."

"All right, Barry. All right. You don't have to beat me over the head with it. I get your point." He must have handed the mike to Bonnie. "What do you want us to do?" she asked.

Cutter reached for the mike. "I'll be more than happy to tell her what to do!"

Laughing, Barry said, "Just hang back and get ready for some more action pics, folks."

A convoy of eighteen-wheelers rolled by on the south side of the divided highway.

"Hey, northbound! How's it lookin' over your shoulder?"

"Haven't seen a thing," Barry radioed. "I been runnin' with an ol' boy since Kansas. I must have run off and left him 'bout ten miles back. Called himself Machine Gun . . ."

Cutter rolled her eyes at that handle.

". . . You hear from him, tell him I'll hook up with him up in Cheyenne."

"Will do. You're clean for another seventy-five miles. I'm the Goatherder."

"They call me the Dog."

A moment of silence. "I heard of you. Goatherder is bye-bye!"

Several miles went by. Barry followed the lights of the lead trucks, both of them leaving the left lane clear.

The drag truck blinked his running lights three times.

"What the hell's he doing?" Barry muttered.

The running lights flickered three more times.

"Maybe he's telling you to go to three," Cutter suggested.

Barry flipped the CB to channel 3 and lifted his mike. "If you got something to say, say it."

"Barry Rivera," the speaker crackled. "The Dog. You're Latino, Dog. You should be on our side, fighting for your oppressed people."

"Pure garbage!" Barry told him.

"You don't believe in helping to lift the oppressed out of starvation and ignorance and easing the yoke of the slave masters."

Barry laughed into the mike. "You bastards have that drivel down pat, don't you? I think you've had it drilled into your heads so much you actually believe part of it."

He turned to Cutter. "Get ready with that forty-four mag. Let's see if we can't put the one right in front of us out of action and then we'll take on number three."

"It isn't drivel, Dog. The Zionists have taken over New York

City. They've driven my brothers and sisters from their home-land and claimed it for their own. You can't deny that."

Barry eased up a few yards, doing it very slowly. "God gave that land to them, you asshole."

Then he lifted the mike to the military radio. "George. Go to channel three on your CB. Do it. Right now." He listened to his CB.

"Are you there, Dog?"

"Right behind you, baby killer."

The laughter was ugly and taunting. "You were in Vietnam, Dog?"

"I was."

"And you call me a baby killer?"

"I killed no babies, Ahmed, or Flannery, or Kurt, or camel-shit, or whatever your name is."

The voice cursed him.

Barry pulled up closer. A few more yards and Cutter could let the hammer down on the big .44 mag with the Teflon-coat ammo.

"He's from the Middle East," Cutter told him. "That accent is unmistakable."

"The ones in the truck back there"—he jerked his head—"were not."

"I know. They're all linked up. And getting worse."

"If I don't kill you, Dog, there are hundreds more just wait-ing for their chance. The price on your head keeps going up and up. And we keep growing and growing, thanks to the ac-tions of your pig president."

"George and Bonnie are probably eating that up," Barry said tightly.

"Loving it for sure," Cutter agreed.

"Who are you?" George's voice cut in.

"Oh, hell!" Cutter groaned.

"He's marking himself." Barry shook his head in disgust.

"Ah! Another voice heard. And who are you?"

"George Stanton . . ."

"That dumb son of a bitch!" Barry shouted.

". . . I'm doing a series on terrorism in the United States. I'd like to talk with you. What is your name?"

"My name is not important. George Stanton. Certainly. I have heard of you, of course. A fair man in your reporting, to be sure."

"Oh, butter him up!" Barry spat the words. "Stroke that monumental ego."

"Thank you. I was on my way to have an interview with Darin Grady."

"Yes. We know. Then you failed to keep it. And now you are traveling with a killer-dog. Curious, to say the least."

"I have to have both sides of the story," George told him.

"That would be a first," Cutter said, disgust in her voice.

Barry nodded his head in agreement. "If the silly bastard isn't real careful, he's going to end up on a hit list."

"Maybe that's the only way the press is ever going to wise up?"

"They've been grabbed before and they haven't seen the light yet," Barry reminded her.

"That is true."

"I think you are a traitor, George Stanton. I think you are probably working for the CIA."

Both Barry and Cutter got a big kick out of that.

"I most certainly am not!" George spoke with real indignation in his voice.

"I think you are a lying Yankee pig! I think your true colors have finally been exposed. You were on your way to kill Darin, weren't you?"

"Don't be absurd, you idiot!"

"I think you will not die well, George."

"Now!" Barry yelled.

Cutter leaned out the window and blew a hole in one back tire of the terrorists' rig. She shifted the muzzle and blew out a fist-sized chunk from a tire on the other side.

The rig slowed. Cutter fired again, missed, and jacked the

hammer back, firing again. With two tires on one side now ruined, the trailer leaned to one side and slowed. Barry swung into the left lane just as Cutter was ramming home fresh rounds from a speed-loader.

She emptied the pistol into the cab of the terrorist rig, not trying to maintain pistol control by shooting through the glass alone, for with the .44 mag and its custom-loads, it could shoot through several inches of solid metal.

Cutter started several feet below the glass and let it bang. The terrorist rig headed for the ditch and stopped abruptly when the tractor impacted with a rock wall.

Barry didn't know if Bonnie was filming or not; if not, she was missing one hell of an opportunity.

One door of the trailer of the last remaining terrorist convoy flew open and the lead started flying from automatic weapons, the slugs whining and howling off the bulletproof metal and windshield of Barry's tractor. Cutter tossed the big .44 mag to the floorboards and grabbed up her CAR, checking to see that the weapon was set on full automatic.

"Careful!" Barry shouted, over the rush of wind coming through her open window.

She opened the side vent wide, shoving the muzzle of the CAR under the bulletproof glass and between the mirror mounts and pulled the trigger, holding it back.

The CAR hammered out its death song, the thirty-round clip quickly emptying.

But she had cleared the trailer door of terrorists. Barry's lights picked up on two bodies, sprawled in death on the trailer floor. The others had ducked behind the dubious protection of the closed door.

Cutter taught them a hard lesson by picking up the .44 mag, loading it full, and blowing jagged holes in the trailer door.

Barry had stayed in the left lane, giving Cutter a better firing advantage, but also exposing George and Bonnie to terrorist fire.

He had hoped they would fall back. They did not. They had

pulled even closer, giving Bonnie better shots with the mini-cam.

The driver of the terrorist truck was trying to escape, but his rig was no match for the custom Kenworth of Barry's.

"Let's take them out, Cutter!" Barry yelled.

She nodded her head and reloaded the big mag.

Barry easily caught up with the terrorist truck and pulled even.

Cutter emptied the .44 mag into the cab as Barry roared past, wanting to be clear as the big rig lost control under the dead hands of the terrorist driver.

The truck abruptly shot to the right and left the interstate, sailing for a few yards, all tires spinning in empty space. It landed hard, the trailer breaking loose from the fifth wheel and rolling, splintering open, spilling bodies as it rolled. The tractor went end over end and landed on its top, steel and glass crushing and tearing anything that might have been left alive in the cab.

Cutter was shaking her right hand, the wrist numbed from the jarring of the .44 mag.

Both Barry and Cutter had ringing ears from the sounds of combat, and rolling up the window helped but a little.

Barry grabbed the mike. "Everything all right back there, George?"

He turned up the volume to compensate for their temporary loss of hearing.

"I . . . guess so," George radioed. His voice sounded a bit shaky.

"What do you mean, you guess so? Is anybody hit?"

"No. No, we're all right. But the windshield has several bullet holes in it. Bonnie got a lot of the action on tape. That man I was speaking with was totally insane!"

"Yeah. You're learning something about terrorists, George. All the gauges reading okay on your Bronco?"

A few seconds of silence. "Yes. Everything appears to be all right."

"Stay with us. We'll stop outside of Denver, before dawn, and I'll take a hammer to that windshield. You can tell the glass replacement people that vandals did a job on you."

"All right. Barry? I made a serious mistake back there, didn't I? Telling that . . . person my name."

"Depends on whether someone ahead or behind was monitoring our transmissions, or whether some of those jerks survived. But I'd say, yeah, you're on a hit list, George. And, George. . . ?"

"Yes?"

"Welcome to the club."

14

Barry and Cutter stayed in the truck parking area and watched as a crew from a glass replacement company out of Denver replaced the windshield in the Bronco.

Then, while Bonnie went to the restroom, Barry took all the cans of film she'd shot.

"You'll get it back," he assured George. "But only after our faces have been censored out. I give you my word on that."

"Oddly enough, I believe you." The reporter lit a cigarette. Barry noticed that his hands trembled slightly. George caught Barry's look and smiled. "You should have seen me a couple of hours ago. This is calm compared to then."

"How did Bonnie take the combat situation?"

"Very well. It didn't seem to bother her. But then, camera-people are a strange bunch to begin with."

Barry laughed and patted the reporter on the shoulder. "You're all right, George. For a liberal," he added, then walked back to his rig.

Air Force special operations people met them in Denver and took both the rig and the Bronco to be serviced and checked and placed under guard. Captain Barnett had checked them into a motel on the outskirts of the city, and met with Barry and Cutter in his room.

"Bonnie O'Neal checks out sort of funky," Barnett informed

them. "She dropped out of college after two years. Then went to work for a small TV station. That's how she got interested in film work. We can't link her to any group with terrorist ties. She's a registered democrat and avowed liberal. Strong Tim Clayton worker; believes in gun control, which is in direct contradiction to your finding that thirty-eight in her gear."

"There appears to be a lot more to Miss O'Neal than meets the eye," Barry said.

"I'm sure you'd be quite the expert on that," Cutter noted.

Barnett looked confused. "I'm missing something here."

Barry waved his hand. "Forget it. Private joke. What's the word on Darin Grady?"

"We believe he's linked up with this Ja person. He's somewhere in California. And Bakhitar has left Chicago and is believed to have joined up with Grady and Ja. My people recovered two live terrorists from last night's attack on you and Cutter. We flew them to an Air Force facility in Nebraska. Under heavy guard. *Our* guards. They won't escape."

"Get anything out of them." Cutter asked.

He shook his head. "No. And don't expect to until they're recovered from injuries and we can shoot them full of joy-juice and question them. Of course that violates their constitutional rights and nothing they say can be used in a court of law. But we didn't expect to try them openly anyway."

Neither Barry nor Cutter had anything to say about that. Both knew that if Captain Barnett could have his way, there would not be any trial at all. The two terrorists would simply disappear.

"Let's get back to Bonnie O'Neal," Barry suggested.

"I'm sure you'd like that." Cutter smiled.

Barry sighed.

Captain Barnett got it then. He grinned at Barry. "The price one must sometimes pay in serving one's country, huh, Dog?"

"You got that right."

Cutter had some choice words to say about that, then calmed

down when Barry and Barnett both began laughing at her antics.

"All right! All right!" she said. "Let me ask you both this: is there a chance Miss O'Neal is a government plant?"

Barnett's eyes narrowed. "Interesting thought. But you don't mean from any agency who would be understanding of what we do, right?"

"Correct."

"Like," Barry mused aloud, "from some rich senator's office. That same senator who just might have presidential aspirations and who would just love to get some dirt about covert activities going on within the boundaries of this country?"

"And who would just love to get some dirt about this mysterious Dog who is a one-man wrecking crew?" Barnett added.

"Bingo!" Cutter said with a frown.

Barnett walked to the door and waved one of his people inside. "Don't let Bonnie O'Neal out of your sight and arrange for someone to put a tap on her phone. Right now! And send Jamison in here."

He turned back to Barry and Cutter. "We're going to have to walk light on this. Senator Tim Clayton is no little known name. And he's got one hell of a campaign going for him. He's a strong presidential contender for next year's election."

"God help the country if he's elected," Barry said. "That son of a bitch will give it away lock, stock, and barrel."

Cutter had picked up the dossier on Bonnie O'Neal. "She worked as a cameraperson in Connecticut and then for a time in Massachusetts. The network picked her up last year. Why would they assign someone with less than a year's experience to do a story with a top-gun name like George Stanton?"

"Maybe because her network makes very little effort to disguise its almost fanatical hatred of our President," Barnett said. "Ever since the President referred to the head of that network's news department as a man with about as much patriotic responsibility as a toadstool, they've been gunning for him."

Barry laughed, remembering the incident well.

And the big flap it had caused.

The head of the news department demanded an apology from the President. The President of the United States told the news head to go suck an egg.

"We're concentrating pretty heavily on Bonnie," Cutter said, grudgingly. "But let's don't forget about George."

"We haven't," Barnett assured her. "But George Stanton is clean. He was raised in a well-off and totally committed democratic-leaning environment. His father was an avowed Republican-hater. George came up the same way. A nonviolent person. He was too young for Korea, and his number never came up for Vietnam. George is slightly pompous, sometimes overbearing, always liberal-leaning in his reporting. But in his own way, he's a very decent and caring person. He contributes heavily to animal-rights organizations, is opposed to laboratory experimentation on animals, helps to support several needy children through contributions . . . that sort of thing. George can be a potatohead, but he's basically all right. Married for eight years. His wife died. Never remarried."

"Brings it back to Bonnie," Barry said.

A knock on the door and Barnett jerked it open, admitting Sergeant Gale.

"One of our people just got this back from Hays," the sergeant said. "That call Bonnie O'Neal made last night? She called Senator Tim Clayton's Washington, D.C. number. Talked for four and a half minutes."

"Thank you, Sergeant."

The sergeant left the room.

"I got an idea," Barry said. "But for it to work, George is going to have to go along with it."

Barnett pulled up a chair. "Let's hear it."

George was appalled. Outraged. Indignant. "That is the most unconscionable thing I have ever heard of. To violate the news in such a manner. I will do my best to have Miss O'Neal dismissed!"

"Oh, settle down, George." Barry stood up. "Hell, I thought you'd be pleased."

"Pleased!"

"Well, you'd get to shaft the administration. That's what you people try to do every time I've ever turned on the news."

George studied him. "That's sad, Barry—that you would feel that way."

"Oh?"

"We just report the news."

"As you see it."

"Ummm! Perhaps. You don't want Miss O'Neal taken off this assignment?"

"No."

"What do you want?"

"I want to set her up."

Cutter snickered. "Or down."

Barry looked at her. Sighed.

"I don't understand," George admitted.

Barry explained.

George smiled. Then laughed. "My father is probably spinning in his grave. But all right, Barry. It'll serve all three of them right. Assuming the news chief is involved. Assuming any of it is true. When does this operation start?"

"It'll take about two days to set it up." He looked at Barnett and received a nod of confirmation. "That'll give us forty-eight hours to rest and relax."

George studied him with cool eyes. "I think, Barry, that I do not ever want you for an enemy."

"That would probably be wise," Barry agreed.

Every move that Bonnie O'Neal was making was being observed. Her room was bugged and her phone tapped. She was covered like a blanket. A lip reader had been brought in if she decided to make a call from a phone booth and the shotgun mikes were unable to pick her up, which was unlikely.

They had all rested, napped, and relaxed the rest of that day. At seven o'clock that evening, Barry knocked on Cutter's door.

Barnett had reserved suites for them all. Very private ones. Seems this particular motel was used by nearly all intelligence-gathering organizations, and the rooms were soundproofed and bug-clean.

Barry was counting on soundproof.

And he would prefer not to have it recorded, either.

Barry had watched room service bring Cutter's dinner to her about an hour earlier. She had obviously just taken a shower and dried her hair.

He wondered if she was wearing anything under her robe.

"Well!" Cutter said. "Isn't this a surprise. You decide to let Bonnie rest this evening?"

She was joking, and Barry knew it. But the joke was beginning to wear a little thin.

"Your bluff is called, Cutter."

"What bluff, Dog?"

He stepped in and pushed her back. She was a big strong woman, and Barry had to put some muscle behind the push.

Her eyes narrowed and her face flushed. She was a dangerous woman, and Barry was fully aware of that fact.

"I call the shots concerning bed partners, Dog!" She spat the code name at him.

"Like I said, calling your bluff."

"No way, Dog!"

Barry laughed and jerked at the sash of her robe. It parted. Underneath—pure Cutter.

She swung at him and he ducked, his right hand shoving out, catching her on the chest and landing her butt-first on the bed.

She kicked at him and he grabbed a bare foot and turned her over, her robe bunching up around her hips.

"You got great buns, Cutter."

She clamped down on his arm with her teeth and drew blood.

He brought the palm of his left hand down sharply on her bare butt and left a red mark.

She yelped and caught him on the side of the head with a fist that knocked him flat off the bed and onto the floor.

He grabbed an ankle and hauled her off the bed, rolling her up in her robe.

"You son of a bitch!" she hissed at him.

No shouting or screaming on her part. Just hitting and kicking and biting. And none of that very serious. Not nearly as seriously as she knew how.

He manhandled her up off the floor and onto the bed, stripping her of her robe along the way.

She was one hell of a magnificent woman, in the absolutely peak of physical fitness.

She lay on the bed, passive, looking up at him.

"You want to fight some more, Cutter?"

"I'd rather not. I wouldn't want to bruise your ego by actually kicking your skinny ass."

He tugged off his boots and in a moment stood naked before her eyes.

Her eyes touched every scar on his muscular body.

He lay down beside her and stroked her flesh. "This is more fun than fighting, isn't it?"

"So far," she said with a sigh.

After a few moments, he parted her legs. "Any suggestions, Cutter?"

She reached out and grasped him.

"Just keep on truckin', Dog," she said.

15

Barry's truck had been replaced by a look-alike Kenworth. It was standard SST. It was still bulletproof and armor plated, but without the hidden compartments in Barry's custom rig. Same color, same make, same model.

"This move is going to break the back of terrorists," Barry told George and Bonnie, knowing that Bonnie knew absolutely nothing about trucks and trailers. "We'll be heading east in twenty-four hours. Inside that specially equipped trailer will be a squad of CIA-trained mercenaries, heavily armed." The trailer was actually filled with government-sealed crates of parts for M-60 machine guns and M-16s. There were five crates of the newly adopted military sidearm: the Beretta 9mm, and crates of holsters for the weapon. And several crates filled with highly classified decoding machines.

"So you're going to lure the terrorists out and then gun them down like vicious animals?" Bonnie asked, her blues bright with anticipation.

"Goddamn right!" Cutter said.

"Fantastic!" Bonnie agreed.

Barry handed her a film box. "Here's the film you took of that firefight the other night, Bonnie. It's intact except for our faces being censored."

"Still shows all the gross stuff? All the shot-up bodies and all that?"

"Certainly," Barry said with a smile. "I told you we'd be fair with you."

"Fantastic!"

What the film held was scenes of truck-driving videos used as a training aid for SST drivers.

"Where do you think the terrorists will hit us, Barry?" George played his rehearsed part like a pro.

"Our intelligence picked up a communique giving us the exact location." He pointed to a map. "Right here. In Kansas." He grinned at Bonnie. "It's going to be a bloodbath, Bonnie. And we're not going to take any prisoners. Those orders come from the President of the United States. We're going to kill them all. Any left alive will be tortured for information."

"Fantastic!" Bonnie's face was looking a little strained.

"Of course, you won't want to see that," Cutter said, straight-faced. "It's very bloody. We use whips and electrical wires to various parts of the terrorist's bodies."

"Right." Bonnie bobbed her head. "I understand."

"Now, Bonnie," George said, a fatherly tone in his words. "This is ultra top secret. None of this can leak out. It would ruin the President's chances for reelection next year, and the party's reputation forever. You understand?"

"Oh, yes, sir, Mr. Stanton." She peered at the map again. Stuck her finger on the spot. "Right there, huh?" She looked at Barry.

"Right there, Bonnie. Once we get past that point, nothing can stop us. The Kansas Highway Patrol will be in on it. They want to kill those sorry bastards, too."

"Right." Goddamn pigs were the same all over the world, she thought. Bloodthirsty savages.

Barry put a hand on her shoulder. "I'm trusting you with top-secret operation orders, Bonnie."

"Oh, you can trust me, Barry."

"Right."

"I have a question." Bonnie moved closer, shoving a breast against Barry's arm.

"Anything, Bonnie. You name it and I'm willing to share it with you."

Cutter almost choked on that.

"Why will we be on secondary roads this time, and not on the interstate."

"Because we want to make it easy for them, Bonnie. We have information that this group will be comprised of young terrorists. A lot of girls involved. Eighteen, nineteen years old. We like to take them that young. They last longer under intense torture. It's a whole lot more fun." He winked at Bonnie. "Some of the mercenaries are really looking forward to taking some of the girls alive. It's a lot of fun to watch. You'll love it."

Bonnie looked like she'd just love to throw up. "So we move out in twenty-four hours, huh?"

"Twenty-four hours on the dot, Bonnie. You'd better get lots of rest. Cutter and I will be getting our rig ready and George will be interviewing this man." Barry indicated an AF man who would soon be on a plane to Greece. "He's in charge of the entire operation. So you'll have the motel to yourself."

Her face brightened. "Oh, I'll be all right, Barry!"

Barry patted her shoulder. "Good. We sure wouldn't want anything to happen to you. You're a real patriotic young lady."

Cutter did her best to keep a straight face.

"We'll take the interstate down to Pueblo and pick up high-way ninety-six east from there," Barry told the group, minus Bonnie. He looked at Sergeant Gale. "You say our Miss Bonnie is burning up the phone lines?"

"If she holds that phone to her ear much longer, she's going to have to have it surgically removed," the sergeant confirmed. "She's called Senator Clayton a dozen times. We've got a tap on Clayton's phone. He's arranging for a very unwelcome welcoming committee to stop your rig right here." Gale marked the spot on the map.

"And she's been in contact with Gene Forbes?" George asked.

"Yes," Gale told him. "The head of your news department is up to his butt in this. He'll be there with bells on, so to speak. Full camera crew. And"—he smiled—"the good senator will also be there. With a speech prepared, condemning the current administration and its horrible, terrible use of mercenaries to kill those wonderful sweet young terrorists. A team from the FBI has been alerted that Clayton's group will be interfering in the transportation of legitimate military hardware. They'll be there, in hiding."

George's smile was hard. "I love it," he said, surprising them all. "I am opposed to the use of force when it is not necessary, but I am adamantly opposed to the news media compromising themselves for a political end. It's positively disgraceful."

None of the military people in the room trusted themselves to respond to that. And neither did Barry. None of them knew quite how to take George's flip-flop.

"Cutter's papers are ready?" Barry asked Barnett.

"She's been an SST driver for two and a half years. The FBI couldn't break her story now."

Barry looked at his watch. After four in the morning. "I'm beat. We pull out in ten hours. I'm hitting the sack."

Barry stood for a time in the cold night air. He had called Jackson, advising him of their plan. Jackson had loved it. All in all, a neat little operation.

Barry was still smiling as he went to sleep.

"You two take off," Barry told George and Bonnie. "We're picking up the mercenaries in Pueblo. We'll meet you at the Kansas state line, on highway ninety-six."

George walked away, toward his Bronco. Bonnie stood for a moment, looking at Barry.

"Something on your mind, Bonnie?"

"We all have to do what we think is right."

"Oh, absolutely. No doubt about that."

"Despite what might happen, Barry, I think you are a very brave man."

"Thank you."

She walked away. Barry watched her go. Still had a great ass.

"Let's roll, Cutter."

Rolling south on Interstate 25, Cutter said, "Are you anticipating any trouble on this run?"

Barry shook his head. "Not until after we kick the slats out from under Forbes, Clayton, and Little Miss Muffet."

"That's the way I see it. Now tell me your reasoning behind that."

"I think the terrorist organizations around the world have a far greater number of supporters and sympathizers in this country than even you people realize. I think they have supporters in government, both elected and appointed, in civil service. They have them in the military, the police. And they've gotten wind that Senator Tim Clayton is about to put the skids under your group and me. The various terrorist groups want to see the U.S. humiliated, worldwide. And Forbes is so goddamn uncaring and Clayton so filled with self-righteousness neither of them know or care that they are playing right into the hands of the terrorists."

"I couldn't have put it better."

"Thank you. It was rather good, wasn't it?"

She muttered something under her breath and rolled her eyes.

Cutter took the wheel at Pueblo and rolled the rig on old 96 over to near the Kansas line. At Sheridan Lake, she turned the wheel over to Barry. A few minutes later, they picked up a tail: George and Bonnie. Barry waved them on ahead.

"I bet Bonnie is beginning to sweat just a little about right now, Cutter. She's beginning to get it through her head that is not the same Bronco."

"She must be stupid."

"No. Just not very observant. Lots of folks look at things but never see them. She saw two radios. She just now figured out they are two CBs."

"Where do you think they'll hit us, Barry?"

"About halfway between Scott City and Ness City. We ought to be hearing something from your people at any moment."

Their military radio began speaking to them about fifteen minutes later.

"Large crowd gathered on the east side of Dighton, Dog."

"Hell, that's Jackson!" Barry said, startled. He picked up the mike. "You here for the show, Jackson?"

"Moral and official support. I am still with Treasury, remember? And we take a dim view of people intercepting shipments of government weapons."

"It's so nice to have you people on our side, Jackson. All your official badges and stuff."

"Don't overdo it, Dog. You're making me ill."

"Tell me what to expect."

"A large crowd of Clayton supporters. Lots of antiwar signs. Looks like something from the sixties."

"Do I have your permission to run over the whole damned bunch of them?" Barry winked at Cutter, anticipating Jackson's reply.

"Jesus Christ, no, Dog! Control yourself. Stick with the original plan . . ." Then he realized Barry was kidding him. "You jerk!"

"Passing through Grigston, Jackson."

"You've got about fifteen miles to go. They'll stop you on the east side of town, about two miles out. All our people are in position. Secret Service is awfully jumpy about this, Dog."

Cutter grabbed the mike. "What in the hell is the Secret Service doing there?"

"Clayton announced his bid for the presidency about six hours ago. In Kansas City."

"But he isn't from Missouri or Kansas."

"Trying hard for the midwest vote. I'm out now, gang. Stay cool and with the plan."

Barry held the rig at a steady 55 mph. He held to the speed limit through the little town of Dighton. On the outskirts of town, they could see the lights of the huge crowd, or mob, waiting for them, blocking the road. Barry brought the rig to a halt and rolled down his window as a Kansas Highway Patrolman walked up to him.

"What the hell's going on, Officer?"

"Beats the hell out of me, driver. About ninety minutes ago I got a call that that presidential candidate, Tim Clayton, was here, with a mob. The secret service is here, all pissed-off and jumpy. Bunch of damn hippies have crawled out of the woodwork and joined in. I thought all those people were *dead!* Or grown up or something."

"I still don't understand what we have to do with Tim Clayton. Hell, I don't even like the bastard!"

"I heard that." He looked up at Barry. "Are you carrying armed mercenaries?"

Barry looked startled. "Mercenaries! Hell, no! I'm pulling for the Transportation Department, U.S. government. We're SST. Taking a shipment of weapons and other materials to Fort Drum, New York."

"Can I see your papers?"

"You sure can."

The crowd had pushed closer, with the KHP leading the way, followed by the secret service, who was followed by a smug-looking Tim Clayton.

Both Barry and Cutter climbed down. The patrolman gave Cutter a startled look, appraised her and gave her a ten and a half, then reluctantly returned his gaze to Barry.

"Is that your partner?"

"Sure is. We've been together for over two years."

"There they are!" Tim Clayton yelled. "Government employed murderers and hit men . . ." He looked at Cutter. ". . . Ah, hit people!"

Camera crews and reporters, from all networks, broke through and crowded around Barry and Cutter and the highway cop.

"That man's a damn fool!" Cutter said, looking at the nattily dressed Clayton. "What the hell is a hit people?"

"Murderers and killers!" Clayton shouted. "The President's goons and stooges. Violations of human rights and constitutional due process. Now you all see to what levels this present administration has dragged the flag . . ."

Someone handed him a bullhorn.

". . . People of America!" Clayton shouted. "Open your eyes and view the horror this administration has sunk to . . ."

"Is that proper English?" Barry whispered to the patrolman.

"I don't think so."

"Friends of humanity and supporters of the democratic way!" Clayton shouted. "Surround this killer truck and help me strip away the evil shrouds of wanton destruction."

Somebody boosted Clayton up onto the hood of the Kenworth and tossed him the bullhorn.

"I have it on the finest information possible," Clayton yelled, "that this truck is carrying armed mercenaries. This truck, and others like it, roam the nation, highway thugs and bullies, picking fights and killing people!"

A collective *OOOHHH* went up from the hand picked crowd.

Barry stepped forward. Bonnie noticed then that he had not shaved in several days, and his was a naturally heavy beard. His face was shadowed. Where he usually wore cowboy boots, he now wore tennis shoes. His cowboy hat had been replaced with a Greek seaman's hat. And he was wearing glasses. She couldn't remember ever seeing him in glasses.

Bonnie O'Neal, super supporter of Tim Clayton, got a sudden desperate feeling that, both literally and figuratively, she'd been had by one Barry the Dog.

"Friends of a free and open America!" Clayton shouted through the bullhorn. "Supporters of due process. Champions of the depressed . . . ah, oppressed, the downtrodden, the homeless, the world's . . . ah . . ."

"Huddled masses?" Barry prompted.

"Shut your goddamn mouth, you . . . you . . . truck driver!"

"I thought I was a baby killer."

"You are!" He lifted the bullhorn to his lips. "Brothers and sisters!" Clayton spoke with reverence in his voice. "Hear my words, all you who have gathered here this momentous evening . . ."

"I lift my lamp beside the golden door," Barry said.

Clayton lowered the bullhorn and glared at Barry. "Will you, for Christ sake, shut your damn face!"

"Hold it!" Jackson's voice came through a bullhorn. "Agent Jackson, Treasury Department. Just stand back and clear a path."

"It's about time," Barry muttered.

16

The crowd parted, reluctantly, and Jackson stepped up to Barry and Cutter and the Kansas Highway Patrolman.

"What the devil is going on here? I was in the pace vehicle with this SST. We lost contact."

"I'm sorry," Barry said. "I had to stop. This mob was blocking the road."

"And that yoyo up there had to make a speech," the KHP said, pointing at Clayton.

Jackson turned to a young secret service agent. "Why has this been permitted? This rig is carrying weapons and decoding equipment to Fort Drum, New York."

"I don't know," the secret service man said, disgust in his voice. "Where he goes"—he jerked his thumb toward Clayton—"we gotta go."

Clayton tried to get down from the hood of the Kenworth and almost fell. Barry and Cutter had to help him down.

"Get your hands off me!" Clayton yelled, shaking them loose once he was on the ground. He faced Jackson and several FBI personnel who had gathered around, including one woman agent. She had looked at Cutter and the women had exchanged winks. "I want you agents to surround this truck and break that seal. This truck is carrying mercenaries."

"Oh, crap!" Barry said. "This rig is sealed. People would die in there. They'd use up the air in less than half an hour."

"You see!" Clayton shouted. "He's afraid to open the trailer

We've got them, people! We've trapped them all in a dirty lie!"

A tremendous roar went up from the crowd.

Barry waited until the cheering had died down. He looked at Clayton. "I can't pop those seals, mister-whoever-you-are. But if this Treasury man or one of these FBI people wants to open it, that's their concern."

"Open the doors!" Clayton roared.

He turned to Jackson. "Are you in charge here?"

"If I were, I'd give you a ticket for obstructing traffic and creating a disturbance."

"Cretin!" Clayton hissed. He turned to an officer of the Kansas Highway Patrol. "Surround the truck!"

"I have no reason to surround the truck, Senator Clayton. It's a *truck*—that's it as far as I'm concerned. I have no evidence to show otherwise and absolutely no right to detain this vehicle."

Clayton looked at one of his secret service guards. "Open the trailer doors!"

"I don't have the right to do that, Senator. We're here to guard you."

"All right, all right!" Jackson stepped in. "I'll take responsibility for breaking the seals." He looked at Barry. "Let me see the manifest."

"He's got them." Barry pointed to the young trooper.

Papers in hand, Jackson moved to the rear of the trailer, the crowd moving with him. The lights from the TV people illuminated the weird scene.

Clayton began jumping up and down. "Draw your guns! Draw your guns!"

"I thought you didn't like guns?" Jackson reminded him.

"This is different. Our lives are at stake here."

"Right," Jackson said.

"Senator Clayton," a reporter from another network asked, "just where did you get your information about there being armed mercenaries in this trailer?"

"From a confidential source. I can't divulge that information."

But he was looking straight at Gene Forbes, who was looking straight at Bonnie O'Neal, who wished the earth would suddenly open and swallow her.

Jackson opened an envelope from the packet he'd taken from the KHP and stepped up to the trailer doors.

"Draw your guns," Clayton screamed. "Everybody get down. Those are mad-dog mercenaries in there. They have nothing to lose. They'll kill us all."

Clayton grabbed the KHP officer by his jacket. "Draw your guns, man!"

Clayton's followers had hit the ground, hiding behind trees, in the ditches, behind vehicles, all with eyes wide.

"Looks like a bunch of owls," the KHP officer commented. "Oh, all right, Senator." He waved to his people. All four of them. "Possible combat situation. But highly unlikely," he added.

The KHP went into a crouch, two-handed grips on their sidearms, pointed at the trailer.

They all felt like a bunch of nuts.

The cameras were rolling, reporters speaking softly into mikes.

Jackson unlocked the trailer doors.

"Careful!" Clayton hollered.

The KHP officer felt he just had to say it, but he felt like an idiot. "You men in there! This is the Kansas Highway Patrol. Come out with your hands in the air."

Silence.

"First one of those crates that talks," Cutter said, to draw attention away from Barry and to herself, "I'm gone, man!"

The reporters all laughed. The secret service laughed. The FBI laughed.

Clayton did not see the humor in it.

Jackson swung the doors open.

Clayton hit the ground, squalling in fright. The TV cameras caught it all.

The floodlights showed carefully stacked and tied-down crates, all government stamped and sealed.

"Now isn't this a crock of shit!" one reporter said.

Clayton, from his prone position on the ground, cut his eyes to Forbes, who cut his eyes to Bonnie, who cut her eyes to George.

Who smiled.

Barry had insisted that Clayton pick out the crates he would like Jackson to open. By this time, the senator had begun to realize all that he had accomplished was to make a total fool of himself.

And he realized something else too: he could hang up his presidential bid.

He had pointed out a crate. Jackson broke the seal and opened the lid. M-16s. Another crate. M-60s. Another crate. Funny looking machines packed carefully against damage.

The press filmed it, packed it up, and left, all of them making jokes about Tim Clayton.

The road was cleared and the KHP pulled out.

Clayton, his press secretary, and his entourage quietly left, the secret service reluctantly going with the senator.

George Stanton looked at Gene Forbes. "You know, of course, the honorable direction to take, don't you?"

"I'll turn in my resignation first thing in the morning."

"Really? I had something more like hara-kiri in mind."

Gene Forbes walked away into the night, got in his car, and drove off.

Jackson stood looking at Barry and Cutter and George, who were all looking at Bonnie O'Neal.

She looked very small and very vulnerable in the night.

"Set me up, didn't you?" she finally said.

"Why the thirty-eight in your luggage?" Barry asked.

"To protect myself against you people, what else?"

"Records show you belong to some coalition to ban handguns," Cutter reminded her.

"That just applies to irresponsible people," she said.

"Sure," Jackson said, relocking and sealing the trailer doors. He tossed the packet back to Barry. The night was very quiet. The townspeople of Dighton had returned to their homes.

"Let's roll," Barry said. "We got a load to deliver."

17

"I can't believe you're letting Bonnie come along," Cutter said, as they rolled eastward. They were angling a bit north, to eventually hook up with Interstate 70.

"I'd rather have her with us, so we can keep an eye on her, than out in public running her mouth."

"I suppose. She sure acted subdued back there."

"It's a total mystery to me why seemingly intelligent people would choose to follow someone like Tim Clayton. The man's a fool."

"A lot of easily led people in the world, Barry. Tim Clayton had never faced much adversity before this night. Now the whole country watched him fold up like a house of cards. We can forget about him."

"I bet she's giving George a hard time of it."

"I wouldn't bet on it, Cutter. George has a hell of a lot more backbone than I'd have ever thought."

"I'm waiting, Bonnie," George said. They were about a half mile behind the 18-wheeler. Barry had radioed back and told them that at Great Bend, they would connect with 156 and take that to Interstate 70.

"I can't believe I've been such a fool," she said softly.

"You want to explain that?"

"Was Clayton drunk tonight?"

"He has a small problem with the bottle, yes."

She fixed eyes on him; hot, young, idealistic eyes. "You mean you knew it all along?"

George shifted uncomfortably behind the wheel of the look-alike Bronco. "We knew that he enjoyed more than his share of the grape, yes."

"How many members of the press suspected it? Or knew of it?"

"Quite a few, dear."

"And you all kept silent about it." Not phrased as a question.

"It was one of Washington's better kept secrets, I will admit that."

"Why, George?"

"I've been asking myself that very question, Bonnie. After Clayton's disgraceful performance this evening."

"I respected you, George. Looked up to you."

"And now you find I have feet of clay. I am sorry."

She pointed to the running lights of the SST. "Those people up there were right, George. The press goes hard on some candidates, easy on others. Am I right, George?"

George said nothing for several moments. "I was never really comfortable with Tim Clayton. Never really sure he was the man for the job. But he stacked up so well against the others. He played well. Always very open with us."

"With the press, you mean?"

"Yes."

"Is that, or should that be a prerequisite for the oval office?"

George sighed. "I suppose not, Bonnie."

"Gene Forbes is through."

"Oh, yes, dear. He's through. He'll turn up somewhere a long way from Washington as some dreary sports announcer for some small-town team. But he'll never again have anything to do with news. Not on a national or international level. He's been made a colossal fool of."

"And Tim Clayton?"

"Don't worry, Bonnie. He doesn't have the courage to kill himself. The people of his state might, probably will, elect him to the Senate again. But it's very doubtful that he'll ever try for any higher office."

"We help to put them up, then we help to tear them down."

"Unfortunately, Bonnie, you are right in that assessment. To a degree."

"I still don't have to like what those people up there"—she pointed to the SST—"are doing."

"You want to quit?"

"No." She twisted in the seat. "George, you're a very smart man. You can be a big windbag at times . . ."

He threw back his head and laughed at that.

". . . But you're very, very intelligent. You know, you *have* to know, that Barry and Cutter and Jackson and the others are never going to let any of this film or commentary about them go on the air."

"Well, of course, Bonnie! Hell, I knew that from the outset."

"But . . . I mean . . ."

"They're showing us a side of terrorism that we've never seen, Bonnie. Their side. No government agent has ever dared do that before. For the simple reason that the high-level people in government, most of them, simply do not trust the press. And," he sighed, "I don't really blame them. We pounce on their mistakes and skim over or completely ignore their many successes. I've been doing a lot of soul-searching these past two days, Bonnie. And I haven't liked a lot of what I've found inside me."

"I've been doing a lot of that same searching for the last hour," she admitted. "I have sort of a bad taste in my mouth."

"Well, we both should, dear."

She again pointed to the lights of the 18-wheeler. "They want you on their side, don't they, George?"

"That's it."

"And. . . ?"

"I don't know, Bonnie. I just don't know."

* * *

Several members of the press dogged the SST for most of the way to Fort Drum, not entirely convinced that perhaps just a part of what Clayton had said that night was true.

Upon orders from Barry, which, surprisingly enough, George followed, he and Bonnie stopped in Missouri and began doing a series of human interest stories. And, since his friends and colleagues all knew that George enjoyed doing a bit of fluff every now and then, no one thought anything about it.

Clayton's fall from grace highlighted the nation's TV screens for a couple of nights, then faded out as other news took its place. Barry was shown along with the story on Clayton, with his Greek seaman's hat and glasses and heavy growth of beard, all of which he had now discarded. But the woman with him remained constantly in the shadows, no camera ever clearly picking up a shot of her.

By the time Barry and Cutter had dropped their load at Fort Drum, they were off the news.

Jackson met them at the Army post. "Your rig is being sent out here by train. Along with the Bronco. And by the way, we've had the Bronco armor-plated and bulletproof glass installed. Since you insist on having those two along. However much the reasoning behind that move might escape me."

"I like their company," Barry said.

"I could add something to that," Cutter said. "But being a lady, I won't."

"Thank you," Jackson said. "You are to both stay here, on the base, and out of sight, for several days. Perhaps as long as a week. We're laying down some rumor-bait and it looks like Ja and Bakhitar and Darin Grady and his bunch are sniffing at it with a lot of interest."

"I know we're the trap, but what's the cheese?" Cutter asked.

"A trailer full of top-secret, handheld, one-man-operated antitank guided weapons. ATGWs. Similar to NATO's Milan system, but these are one-person operated. Any terrorist group in the world would love to get their nasty fingers on something like that."

"We can't run empty, Jackson," Barry said. "One or more of these groups might have people employed by the weight-watchers, and empty would tip our hand."

"Good point. The weight of each launcher, including missile, is 41 pounds. Say ten to twelve pounds for the crate. I'll get on the weight problem right away."

Barry poked him in the belly with a finger. "You are getting a tad soft, Jackson."

"Don't I know it?"

Barry and Cutter lounged in their quarters for several days, keeping a low profile, for the most part staying out of sight, eating and sleeping and catching up on rest.

Barry's Kenworth was shipping in by train and when it arrived, along with the Bronco, Barry carefully went over the rig, from front bumper to the trailer's doors. The twin Harley motorcycles were still in place, carefully strapped down. The crates containing the lethal hardware were intact, and everything was in place in the hidden compartments.

George and Bonnie were flown in, after submitting their human interest stories and George announcing that he was taking a couple weeks' vacation.

Barry put them both through several days of weapons training, with the M-16 and the Beretta pistol, and much to the surprise of both Barry and Cutter, George took to it like that much talked about duck to water.

"This is good fun!" the nationally known reporter said, after blowing the center out of a target with the Beretta.

Bonnie, unfortunately, turned out to be one of those people who could not hit any part of a barn even if she was standing in the center of it.

"Have you ever fired that thirty-eight you're packing around?" Barry asked her.

She had not.

"Who loaded it for you?"

"I did! I mean, any fool can see you just take those bullets and poke them into the holes in that wheel thing."

Barry took the .38 away from her and gave her a can of mace to carry around.

"Thank you," George said. "I feel much better now."

"Don't we all," Cutter told him.

Walking with Bonnie, on a cold and crisp fall afternoon, Barry said, "I thought you'd be so angry you'd never want to see any of us again."

"That was my first thought back there in Kansas while you were making a fool out of Senator Clayton."

"I didn't make a fool out of him, Bonnie. He did all that himself. Forget him, Bonnie. He is not the person to lead this country."

"I realize that, too. Now."

"It's a confusing time, isn't it?"

"Yes." She looked at him as they walked along a path in the sprawling military base just a few miles from the Canadian border. "Who are you, Barry?"

"Who I am is not important. What I'm doing is the important thing."

"No family?"

"No. None. Anywhere." That was a lie. Barry did have a sister still alive in South Texas. But she thought him dead. And that was the way it had to be.

Forever.

"So you just drive around the country, fighting terrorists?"

He took a chance. "For this brief period, yes. Perhaps that's what I'll be doing from now on. I don't know."

"And Cutter."

"She'll return to her job after this trip, probably."

"And you'll be alone?"

"I have a dog. A Husky."

"What's his name?"

"Dog."

She laughed in the cold air and they walked on in silence. Barry's thoughts were spun back in time, back to that truck stop . . .

"Oh, Barry!" Kate said. "Look!" She pointed.

The mutt sat by the Kenworth as if it had found a home. But it did not wag its tail at their approach.

Barry looked at the animal. It was a mixed breed but with the Husky in it predominant. He decided that somewhere down the line, the animal's ancestors, and not too far back, had bred with wolves. He had all the Husky markings, but with the eyes and snout of a wolf. And with the teeth of a wolf.

Kate knelt down and held out her hands. "Come on, boy," she urged.

The animal came to her, allowing the little blonde to pet him.

"What's that on his collar?" Barry asked.

Kate loosened the string holding the worn piece of paper. "A note." She read it aloud. "Goddamn dog bites. You find him, you can have him. He's two years old. Shots are due in the fall. I called him Dog."

Barry knew there was no point in trying to dissuade Kate. Dog had found a home.

"Keep him up here with us until we can find a place to bathe him," Barry told her, once in the rig. "He's got fleas."

Kate ignored that and put Dog in the sleeper.

"Thanks," Barry said.

At a small town, they stopped at a vet's office and had Dog bathed. Dog tolerated it without making a fuss.

"Got some wolf in him," the vet observed. "And a mean look about him. I should have muzzled him, I suppose, but he seems to be taking it all in stride."

Dog was weighed. Sixty-five pounds.

Kate bought a case of Alpo, a water pan, and food dish, and a container to carry extra water. Dog jumped up on the custom bunk in the sleeper and settled right in.

"I think he was raised in a rig," Kate said. "He sure seems to know his way around in a cab."

"I wonder if he can drive." Barry asked.

Dog shifted his cold yellow eyes toward Barry.

"Just kidding," Barry muttered.

"You were a long way from this place, Barry," Bonnie's voice jarred him back to the present.

He nodded his head. "Yeah. I was for a fact."

"Thinking of someone special?"

"My wife. She's dead."

"I'm sorry, Barry."

"Yeah. So am I."

Jackson met with Barry and Cutter, Bonnie and George. The Treasury agent looked at the reporter and the cameraperson. "Once you two get on the road, you realize that you are both fair game for the terrorists. Not just for this run, but for the rest of your lives."

"We understand," George said.

Bonnie nodded her head.

"It's going to be a long run, gang," Jackson continued. "Three thousand miles. Our intelligence shows that the terrorists are coming after this load, foaming at the mouth." He looked at Barry. "They want you dead, in the worst way."

Barry smiled. "What else is new?"

Jackson looked at Cutter. "They want you alive." His words were flat.

Cutter's beautiful face did not change expression. "I can't for the life of me imagine why."

Jackson looked at Bonnie. "I won't mince words with you, Miss O'Neal. These people take you alive, they'll rape you, they'll torture you. Understand all that now?"

"I understand it. I didn't believe it before. But I do now. I'll turn any film I shoot over to you. Perhaps that will help in tracking down any survivors and in studying the terrorists' tactics."

Jackson smiled. "It would be a big help, and we thank you for that."

George said nothing, his silence stating his noncommitment. For now, at least.

"When do we pull out?" Barry asked.

"Oh-six hundred tomorrow morning."

Barry smiled.

All noticed that the peeling back of his lips resembled a vicious snarl.

The Dog had picked up the scent.

18

It was six o'clock and pitch dark when the Kenworth rolled out of the west gate of Fort Drum. They would hook up with highway 26/11 south, take that into Watertown and then pick up Interstate 81 and head south.

Behind them, the Bronco followed, Bonnie at the wheel. In the rear of the Bronco were two M-16s, covered with a blanket, and a bag of full clips. George wore a 9mm in a shoulder holster. The man had turned into a modern-day Wild Bill Hickock.

But whether he could let the hammer fall on a man was yet another story Cutter and Barry could but ponder on.

Cutter was doubtful that he could. Barry was holding judgment. He had a hunch George would come through in a tight spot.

But he hoped it wasn't any of their butts on the line when George had to make that decision.

Both felt it would be a milk run down to Pennsylvania, where they would hook up with Interstate 80 West. The terrorists knew that both Barry and Cutter were heavily armed and would not hesitate a half second to use any weapon at their disposal. They would be very wary about attacking them, and this area was much too populated.

And the terrorists would also know the custom Kenworth, more than $900,000 worth of truck, was thickly armor plated and any conventional hijacking was impossible. And since the terrorists wanted the cargo intact, the use of rockets would be ruled out—too much danger of the fuel blowing and taking the trailer with it.

And there were other points that Barry and Cutter had very carefully gone over with Jackson and George and Bonnie: the terrorists had tried repeatedly to run them off the road. They had failed every attempt, with a heavy loss of life. Being terrorists, the end justified any means. Barry had no family to worry about; that could not be said for any of the others.

George had been appalled. "Are you saying that the terrorists might actually think of doing harm to my *mother!* Good Lord, man! The woman is nearly seventy!"

Cutter had shaken her head at the man's naivete. Barry had sighed and said, "George, you told me you'd been in Lebanon. Tell me what you saw over there. Or did you just look at the scenes without them really registering in your brain?"

"But that was over *there!* This is America. We have laws and rules and . . ."

"Damn it, George!" Barry roared at the man. "When in God's name are you going to climb down off that lofty moral perch you've placed yourself on and tell the American people what terrorism is all about and support this government's efforts to fight it?"

George had fixed his semifamous steely look on Barry. It was wasted. Barry had never been intimidated by any member of the press and damn few other people in his life. George dropped his gaze.

"That's what you want from us, isn't it, Barry? You want the press—the national press, especially the broadcast media—to take a hard-line stance against terrorism."

"That's right, George. You're right."

"You want us to advocate and give our blessings to a no-holds, kick, gouge, bite and stomp, gutter type of warfare against the world's terrorist groups!"

"That's right, George!"

"It'll never happen."

"Why not? Terrorism—unchecked—is going to touch hundreds of lives in every country of the world. Men, women, kids. Young or old. George, I am fully aware that the majority of the press will never go for what I'm advocating. But if just a few would stand up and say: 'We've had it! That's it! We're urging the world's law enforcement personnel and military forces to fight the terrorists in the same manner as they wage war against the innocents of this world: down in the gutter, using gutter tactics.' "

George grunted. A smile had played across the man's lips. "You should have been a politician, Barry. You're very convincing. But the answer is still no. I am going to file a report on terrorism in this country, and it's going to be a hard-nosed look at it. But I will *not* sanction lawlessness to combat lawlessness!"

Barry looked at him, a smile on his lips. "Then why don't you go public with what Cutter and me are doing?"

George had walked away.

Jackson had said, "The Air Force has already assigned people to keep an eye on Cutter's family. I'll arrange for people to keep an eye on George and Bonnie's close relatives!"

"It won't be enough, Jackson."

"I know it."

"Don't you believe for an instant the terrorist groups working in America haven't pinpointed George and Bonnie's relatives for strikes."

"I am fully aware of that, Dog."

"You sure have started taking a hard line during the past ten days," Cutter noted.

"Yeah," Jackson said. "I didn't tell either of you. My oldest kid's in the Navy. Was in the Navy. He was in a cafe in Manila when it was hit by terrorists. Looked like he was going to make it. He died four days ago."

They linked up with Interstate 80 and rolled west. In Ohio, the Interstate system got all screwed up. Interstate 80 melted into nothing and changed to 76. A few miles later, 76 just quit and 71 took its place.

"What the hell happened to the interstate system around here?" Bonnie radioed.

"I don't know," Barry said. "Maybe they changed engineers."

"Ought to be a story in there somewhere." George took the mike.

"When you get through with this one."

"That's a big ten-four!" the nationally known TV commentator laughed.

They rolled on through the night, hitting snow just west of Akron.

"The hell with this!" Barry said. "I'm heading south."

When 76 died an unnatural death, Barry headed south on 71, rolling through the early morning hours. He edged south and west, taking numerous two-lanes, toward Dayton. It was slow going, the snow still hanging with them, mixed with freezing rain.

Barry radioed Wright-Patterson AFB and told security they were coming in for some rest and food.

Security waved them on through and they followed a Jeep to temporary quarters and some hot showers and hot food.

Cutter shook him awake some seven hours later.

Barry was instantly awake. "What's the matter?"

He was reaching for his jeans and boots.

Cutter shoved him back down on the bed. "Nothing's the matter." She slipped into bed with him. "Now."

"Don't look so damned smug," Barry told her.

They were heading south, to eventually hit Interstate 40 and take the southern route to the coast. The weather reports stated that a massive storm was nearly paralyzing everything north and west of Arkansas.

"I'm not smug. Just content."

"Don't get emotional about me, Cutter," Barry warned her. "You're playing a dangerous game."

She shifted in the custom seat and stared at him. "I'm career Air Force, Barry. I'm going to stay with special ops just as long as they'll have me. And I'm going to stay single. So relax."

Barry allowed himself a smile. "And enjoy?"

"You certainly seemed to."

"I can't argue that."

Still snowing but not sticking, and the further south they rolled, it was less snow and more rain. Weather reports stated it was a massive front, and it was stalled, producing snow and rain from California to Ohio.

"How long is this mess going to last?" Cutter asked.

"A couple of days, at least. Maybe longer. Yeah. I know what you're thinking: ideal weather for a strike."

Cutter looked at a road sign. "I seem to recall there are some lonely stretches between Nashville and Memphis."

"There's a dandy stretch of interstate right up ahead." They were just a few miles north of the Daniel Boone National Forest. "About twenty-five miles of nothing." His eyes flicked to his mirror. "And that damn van is still hanging back behind George."

"How long's it been back there?"

"I picked it up just south of Lexington. But I can't tell how many people are in it."

Cutter lifted the mike to the military radio. "George? See if you or Bonnie can tell how many people are in that van behind you."

"I spotted it some time back," Bonnie radioed. "A driver and a passenger is all I can make out. Both men."

"Tell her we're pulling over to the shoulder. They do the same. Let's see what happens."

Nothing. The van rolled on past. Neither man looked at the Kenworth as they drove by.

"Could be something, could be nothing." Cutter vocalized

the frustration. "And with those damned smoked windows I couldn't tell if there was anyone else in the van."

Barry waited for fifteen minutes, parked alongside the Interstate. George eased the Bronco up close and he and Bonnie got out, climbing up into the truck and sitting on the big bunk in the sleeper.

The temperature was falling fast and the weather was turning just plain lousy. Rain lashed at the truck and visibility was dropping fast.

"The problem with being bait," Bonnie said, "is that you never know when the rat is going to try to steal the cheese."

"Or how," Cutter added.

The two women had been getting along better, or at least trying to.

"If that van held hostiles," Barry said, "I think they'll hit us just up ahead." He twisted in the seat and looked at Bonnie. "You drive the Bronco, Bonnie. I want George free to lend us a hand if it comes to that. And it probably will, for you both are marked as being with us. But I warn you now: if you have any doubts, get clear and stay clear. If you exchange lead with these people, they'll mark you down as their enemy, now and forever."

"We'll be right behind you," Bonnie said.

George and Bonnie back in their Bronco, Barry said, "Take the wheel, Cutter. I got a bad taste in my mouth about this."

They pulled out onto the slab. There was no other traffic. The police band scanner's red light stopped.

"Couple of eighteen-wheelers jackknifed on Seventy-five," the voice of dispatch said. "Mt. Vernon exit. Southbound traffic is blocked."

That exit was just about two miles behind them.

Cutter smiled grimly. "How convenient!"

Barry picked up his Uzi and chambered a round. "Let's take it to them, Cutter."

19

Bonnie had picked up the same state police transmission on her scanner.

Her eyes widened as she watched George twist in the seat and pick up one of the M-16s from the rear. "We're press, George! We're here to report the news, not make it, remember?"

George filled the chamber with a live one and set the fire selector switch on rock and roll. "I also have this quaint desire to stay alive, Bonnie. I think it would be very difficult to report the news from the grave."

"You've made up your mind, haven't you?"

"No. I have not. Drive, Bonnie."

The rain was whipping down in heavy sheets, the wipers on both 18-wheeler and Bronco set on full speed as the small convoy rolled along at 40 mph.

"We're looking at about ten or twelve miles of nothing," Barry said. "They'll hit us any second." He had slipped into rain gear and lowered his window. "Get in the left lane and advise Bonnie to do the same."

"I'm sitting here with a madman!" Bonnie said, after receiving the transmission. "He's sitting in the back with the rear window lowered. He's armed himself with a machine gun!"

Both Barry and Cutter grinned. "He's coming around,"

Barry shouted, over the rush of wind and rain through the open window.

Cutter nodded. "Right up ahead, Dog."

Two 18-wheelers had formed an upside-down V in the road. The slab and both shoulders were blocked.

"Eighteen-wheeler coming up fast behind us!" Bonnie radioed. "It's straddling the line, blocking both lanes."

"Put that Bronco in four-wheel drive and jump the median!" Barry radioed. "Get the hell out of here, you two!"

"Sorry," Bonnie returned. "Your transmission is garbled. I can't read you."

Barry tossed the mike in Cutter's lap and cursed. "They're in it, now."

"Their choice," Cutter reminded him.

She slowed the rig and grabbed up the mike. "We have to stop, Bonnie. We can't ram through. Get ready to hit the floorboards or jump."

A man dressed in raingear stepped out from behind one of the trailers blocking the slab and leveled an AK-47 at the Kenworth.

Barry leaned out the window and doubled him over with fire from the Uzi. Cutter had grabbed up her CAR and lowered the window. Behind them, they could hear the sounds of gunfire.

"We're being fired on!" Bonnie's voice screamed through the speaker, and behind her voice, the sounds of George's M-16 barked in three-round bursts.

Slugs flattened and bounced off the windshield of the Kenworth as Barry and Cutter pulled their heads back and waited out the return fire.

Behind them, George and Bonnie dove out of the Bronco as the rogue 18-wheeler came barreling toward them. They got out just in time, rolling off the shoulder and into a deep ditch. The Bronco was rammed and knocked spinning into the median. George leveled his M-16 and made a big mess inside the cab of the offending truck. George felt slightly sick at his stomach as blood splattered the interior of the cab.

He quickly got over his fear as automatic weapons fire kicked up dirt and gravel into his face. He rolled to one side, shoving Bonnie's face down into the wet grass, getting her out of harm's way, and then leveled his M-16 and let the slugs howl and bounce off the concrete. The raincoated terrorist ducked back behind the protection of his rear trailer tires.

"Move! Move!" Barry heard one of the terrorists on the south end yell. "Cops coming."

"Let them go," he told Cutter. "We don't need the heat right now."

"Speak for yourself!" she said with a grin, her face and hair slick with rain. "I'm freezing!"

Barry had jerked the plates off the Bronco and blew the VIN into shreds with his Uzi. He blew the radios to shattered bits with another burst. He had tossed the gear inside the Bronco to George and Bonnie told them to get the hell into his rig and get gone. He'd follow in the terrorist's rig and catch up with them.

The entire operation had taken less than a minute. But in that minute, the rigs blocking the southbound side of the slab had pulled out, both of them running empty and both of them letting the smoke roll.

Barry climbed into the cab of the big Mack and shoved the dead driver to the floorboard. He fell with a dull thud on top of the shot-up codriver. Barry pulled out as fast as he could, straining to see through the blood-splattered windshield. He could see the red lights of the cop cars reflecting off the rain in the distance. He was running without lights, trying to get a tree-lined section of the median between the lanes before he pulled even with the several cop cars.

He just made it, and began breathing a little easier. He cut on his lights and blinked his headlights four times at Cutter;

a prearranged signal to go to channel two on the CB. He reached for the mike. It was gone. Shot all to hell by .223 fire.

One of the terrorists groaned on the floor, startling Barry, for the man had what appeared to be a massive head wound. But the rain pouring through the shattered window had cleaned the wound, and Barry could see he was only nicked on the forehead.

Barry reached down and busted him on the back of the head with his Beretta and dropped the man back to sleep.

Barry put the juice to the Mack and pulled ahead of Cutter, swinging in and flickering his running lights.

They rolled on through the driving rain and occasional bits of sleet. Barry saw no more of the terrorists' rigs; either they were running wide open, which he doubted, or more the case, they had exited off onto 150 and were paralleling Barry and Cutter.

He guessed the man he'd gut-shot had been picked up by his buddies, for he had not seen him back on the road.

He cursed. Nameless people. Faceless people. It was worse than 'Nam.

He found a rest area and signaled Cutter he was turning in. He was wearing gloves so he was not worried about leaving any prints in the Mack. He took the wallet from the dead man and then motioned for Cutter to pull up even with him. In the driving cold rain, they muscled the unconscious terrorist into the Kenworth. It was getting crowded.

"I'll tie him up," Barry said. "Let's get rolling. George, up front with Cutter and keep that M-sixteen ready. Come on, Bonnie, help me roll this bastard over on his stomach and you hold his wrists together."

Using tape from the first aid kit, Barry trussed him up and left him on the floor. "Soon as I get out of these bloody clothes, Cutter, we'll switch places and you can dry off and get into warm clothing, then George and Bonnie. We'll get rid of these bloody muddy clothes down the line."

It was awkward, and there was no space for modesty, but all got dried off and changed. By that time, they were into Tennessee, Barry was behind the wheel, and Knoxville was not far off.

The terrorist was awake and watching them, his eyes filled with hatred, no fear in them.

"When we get to Knoxville," Barry said, "call your people, Cutter. Tell them to get here as fast as possible. We got a live one!"

The terrorist cursed Barry's back.

He was young, in his mid-twenties, but his eyes were old.

Bonnie had dropped the leather curtain and had filmed the young man. He cursed her.

"Bitch-whore! We'll see how you can scream someday!"

She was recording it all.

"It'll be your turn first, buddy-boy," Cutter warned him, real menace in her voice.

The terrorist twisted on the floor and stared at Cutter. "Ah, yes. The Air Force Captain!" He laughed at the surprise that leaped into her eyes at the mention of her promotion.

"You see, Captain Cutter, we know all about your special operations team—or teams, I should say!" His eyes flicked over her, as much of her as he could see. "You're a big strong woman. You'll be able to take a lot of pain!"

Cutter offered no reply.

The terrorist looked at George, sitting on the bunk. "Mr. George Stanton. Your family will pay and pay dearly for your becoming involved with murderers and thugs!"

"I will say this about that." George stared at him, his voice flint hard. "You do not want the media down on you. You really do not want the media to come out hard against you and your ilk!"

The terrorist laughed. "Don't be foolish, you silly man. The American reporters will never advocate dealing with us the way the Dog here does!"

Keep talking, punk, Barry thought. Let your mouth dig your own grave.

But the terrorist shut up and would say no more.

On the outskirts of Knoxville, Barry pulled into a motel and found a place to park around back. He came in through the rear, so no one at the desk could see he was in a truck.

Four people in one 18-wheeler would arouse suspicion.

And one trussed-up terrorist that Barry hoped to God nobody would spot.

Barry checked them in, renting four rooms, telling the desk clerk the others in his party would be along shortly. They were ceasing their travel due to the bad weather.

The clerk thought that was a smart move.

One by one, the others entered the lobby and picked up their room keys.

Barry jerked the terrorist to his feet and helped him out of the cab of the Kenworth. On the blacktop, he pressed the muzzle of the 9mm against the man's backbone. "If you yell, the slug will cut your spine, and I'll leave you to rot on the parking lot. The choice is yours."

"Ruthless bastard!" the terrorist spat out the words, standing in the wet, stormy, and cold night. "As you wish, Dog."

"Move!" Barry prodded him with the muzzle. They walked across the lot. "You got a lot of nerve calling me ruthless."

"You don't understand what we are fighting for."

"Neither do you. None of you people do. You've all lost sight of decency. All you want to do is kill."

"Not true. We fight for a better world."

Barry unlocked the door and shoved the terrorist inside, closing the door behind him, making certain it was locked. "Better world, my ass," he muttered.

Cutter was arranging for a rental car and would travel to a nearby shopping mall to get clothes for the man; all that after she called her people.

The terrorist watched as Barry opened a suitcase and took out a .22-caliber auto-loader, with a long silencer screwed into the barrel. He sneered at Barry. "And you have the nerve to call me a thug and a killer!"

Barry smiled at him. "I also have the nerve to kill you where you sit unless you shut your damned mouth."

The terrorist locked eyes with the man known as the Dog. "I believe you," he said softly. "I will say no more."

The minutes ticked by in silence, the stillness broken only by the still-driving rain hammering at the outside. A knock on the door.

Barry walked to the door. "Yes?"

"Cutter."

He opened the door and she slipped in, several packages in her hands. She dumped those on the bed and turned to face Barry. "I have people on the way. They'll be here in a couple of hours, max. You take a shower and warm up. I'll watch this creep."

Barry didn't need a second invitation. He hit the shower and adjusted the water as hot as he could stand it. He dried off and walked back into the room in his underwear shorts.

The terrorist's eyes took in the numerous scars on Barry's body. Bullet and shrapnel and knife souvenirs. "May I, too, be afforded the luxury of bathing?" he asked.

Barry dressed before replying. "Go ahead." He lifted the muzzle of the silenced auto-loader. "Just bear in mind that a body falling in a tub doesn't make much noise. And the spray will wash away the blood. That would be so much easier than having to explain blood on the carpet."

"I get the message."

Cutter removed the tape from the man's wrists and he carefully stretched, flexing his hands, restoring some lost circulation.

"Strip," she told him.

The terrorist smiled. "Wanting a quick peek at what you are someday going to get, Captain?"

Cutter hit him with a balled fist and knocked the man sprawling, surprise in his eyes at the power behind the punch.

Cutter glared down at him. "The only thing I want from you, punk, is silence!"

Blood leaked from the terrorist's busted mouth. He slowly nodded his head in understanding.

"Get up, strip, and take your bath," Cutter told him.

Barry stood by the open bathroom door, the silenced autoloader in his right hand. He smiled back at Cutter. "Getting a bit testy, aren't you, Cutter?"

"I keep thinking about Jackson's son, sitting in that cafe, minding his own business, and then the room exploding. All because of sorry bastards like that!" She jerked her thumb toward the bathroom.

"It does make it a bit more personal, doesn't it?"

20

They ordered food sent in, and because Barry's room was a divided suite—it was the last room available at the motel—George and Bonnie joined them. The terrorist, bathed and dressed in new clean clothes, sat in the small powder room, adjoining the bathroom, eating his meal, someone always watching the small room with one way in and one way out.

George clicked on the TV, to watch local and national news.

". . . and Kentucky authorities are puzzled over what they now believe was a staged accident on Interstate seventy-five earlier this afternoon," the anchorperson said. "Kentucky State Police report finding numerous shell casings from what they believe to be automatic weapons. The shell casings were found several miles south of the accident site. In the median area, a wrecked four-wheel-drive vehicle was found. No license plates and the vehicle identification number had been shot out.

"About thirty miles south of that scene, an eighteen-wheeler was found parked in a rest area, the driver shot to death, his wallet taken. Authorities are investigating!"

The national and international news was just as boring and depressing and lopsided as it always was. But a self-styled poet did comment about the snow in New York City that covered the flowers in the park.

In rhyme.

"Well," Cutter said sarcastically, "I guess that pretty well covers the important news of the day!"

George and Bonnie said nothing.

The terrorist could not stop his laughter.

Barry looked at him.

"You see?" the young man said with a philosophical shrug of his shoulders. "It is as we already know. Do not think us fools. We have studied and researched your news media. We know what news they'll report and what they will not report—and much more importantly, how they will report it!"

"Yeah," Barry said, pushing his plate from him. "I'll give you that much."

George looked at his watch. "They spent twelve minutes commenting on a Senate hearing that the majority of the American public really doesn't give a damn about. We isolate ourselves—some of us, certainly not all. And we do all sorts of so-called comprehensive and exhaustive research that tells us what the average American wants to see on the news. Then when I speak with that so-called average American, he or she tells me they've stopped watching the news because we run practically the same stories night after night, over and over, and seldom report anything they care to watch because, at least in their minds, it does not pertain to them."

The terrorist was smiling. "The watchdog of the world," he sneered. "The conscience of the nation!" He laughed aloud. "Keep up the good work!"

George rose with a sigh and walked outside, to stand under the awning, breathing deeply, watching the rain as it slashed the earth.

The special operations team came and went with the terrorist. It took less than thirty seconds from the time they pulled in to when they pulled out. One whispered briefly to Cutter and then they were gone.

"What'd he say?" Barry asked, quickly adding, "If it's any of my business, that is!"

"He said for us not to worry about the Bronco. I should

have told you; it just slipped my mind. Nothing about that Bronco is original equipment. When we get them, we switch everything around. The engine, the transmission—anything we can switch, we do, usually. That way, they can be abandoned and as long as the plates are off, we can just say it's another government vehicle that somebody stole a time back." She grinned.

"Cute. But doesn't that get expensive."

"No. They're usually piles of junk when we get them anyway. You're ex-special troop. You remember how a lot of the big brass feels about us. When it's worn out, they give it to us. Screw 'em!"

Barry laughed at her. He remembered only too well. "George and Bonnie?"

"What do you think?"

"I think it's just too dangerous for them to stay with us. I'm going to suggest they pack it in. And I'm going to suggest that they continue with their bodyguards. I really don't think they fully understand—either of them—how much danger they're in."

"I agree with you. And something else: George isn't talking about it, but I think that combat situation back up the road is really bothering him. He'd never killed a man before today."

Barry nodded his head in understanding. "Yeah. He feels pretty bad about it. But he came through. He reached down inside himself and found a deep pool of courage. I don't mean to imply that he'll be a better man because he killed. But he'll be a better person with the knowledge that when push came to shove, he stood his ground and refused to quit."

Barry looked outside. The rain had stopped. He turned back to Cutter. "I'll tell George and Bonnie to stay here, and tomorrow, fly back to New York. Pack it up, Cutter. We're pulling out."

* * *

Barry had made no attempt to conceal his pulling out or the direction taken. He caught up with Interstate 40 and pointed the big steel-reinforced, armor-plated nose of the Kenworth west.

Cutter was asleep in the bunk, the blanket pulled up to her nose.

Barry's Uzi was on the seat beside him, the fire selector set on full rock and roll. His model 92S Beretta was snug in its shoulder holster. He turned on the radio and settled in for a long run.

The highway sang to him as he rolled on; already the road was almost dry. He kept the CB turned down low, so it would not disturb Cutter. Occasionally, he would talk to a trucker; but since he was becoming so well known, he did not use his handle of Dog.

He called himself, with a small smile on his lips: Loup. And the truckers, to a person, or so they said, thought he was referring to a loop as in rope. But he had known many truckers who spoke several languages, and felt sure a lot of them knew that loup meant wolf in French.

He was fifty miles west of Nashville when Cutter crawled out of the bunk and slid into the seat beside him. She picked up the thermos and shook it. "Fresh?"

"Was back in Knoxville," he said with a grin.

"Yukk!"

"First stopping place we'll pull over. For some reason, I'm hungry!"

"I could use a bite myself. Seen anything suspicious?"

"Nothing. I think the bully-boys have realized they've taken on a foe this time who doesn't play by the rules. They've pulled back and are giving this some serious thought."

"You think they've given up on us?"

"No. I think that we've become a direct challenge to them. And now that they know the news media is, or was, traveling with us, they might be thinking that the media will be coming out strong against terrorism around the world. And that's got them worried. They know the military has special operations teams working. And"—he glanced at her in the glow of the dash lights—"you people have a leak."

"Yes. I told my people that on the phone. It'll be plugged, you can bet on that."

"It better be, Cutter. It's your life and the lives of your buddies that are on the line."

"And yours," she gently reminded him.

"When I took this job, I knew that up front. Truck stop up ahead. You go in and get us some coffee and sandwiches. I'll stay with the rig until you get back, then I'll go to the john."

Barry got a little antsy after fifteen minutes had passed with no sign of Cutter returning. After twenty minutes, he was pacing around the truck. When thirty minutes had gone by, he waved to an attendant at the pumps.

"Yes, sir?"

Barry held out a fifty-dollar bill. "Can you stay free of those pumps for thirty minutes and watch this rig?"

"Man, yeah! Just let me holler at Dave."

"This is a government load. Anybody starts hanging around this rig, you start yelling for help, understood?"

"Yes, sir." The fifty-dollar bill vanished in the man's pocket. "You take your time. Take all the time you need."

Barry walked swiftly across the asphalt and stepped into the brightness of the restaurant. His eyes swept the area. No Cutter. He stepped up to the cashier.

"Yes, sir?"

"A lady came in here about thirty minutes ago. Tall, very pretty. Had a thermos in her hand." He hesitated, then took a chance. "We were supposed to meet some people in here. Have you seen her?"

"Oh, sure! She went out the back way about ten minutes ago. With four guys and a lady. She'll be back though."

"How do you know?"

She pointed to a thermos sitting on a counter. "She forgot her coffee."

"Thanks."

"Don't mention it."

Barry did not go out the back way. Instead, he walked out the front and slipped around the east side of the huge building. He moved silently through the rumbling banks of 18-wheelers, their drivers either asleep in the bunks or inside the cafe, eating and drinking coffee and talking.

Barry paused and reached down inside his right boot, extracting a knife from its clip-on sheath. The knife was more a dagger, double-edged, razor sharp. He moved out, staying close to the rigs, staying in the shadows, a hunter/killer on the stalk.

Then he spotted the four-wheeler parked among the rigs. He could see two people inside the car. He recognized the profile on one of them as Cutter. She was sitting on the passenger side. A man sitting behind the wheel. Barry could not tell if anyone was in the backseat.

His eyes roamed the darkness, picking out two men standing in the shadows of 18-wheelers. Very faint light gleamed off the honed blade of Barry's dagger.

A whisper came out of the darkness, from the cab of the rig he was standing by.

"You lookin' for your lady, buddy?"

"Yeah," Barry whispered. "Tall, dark-haired, beautiful."

"Figured you was. She was cussin' up a storm when they passed here. Looked like to me she had a gun shoved in her back. You got a handle?"

"Dog," Barry growled.

The driver caught his breath. "I heard of you. The government, ain't you?"

Barry said nothing; had not even looked up at the man.

"Man and a tough-bookin' broad prowlin' the lot. They look like they know what they're doin'. If you know what I mean. And they talk funny. Foreigners, I think."

"Thanks."

"What can I do to help?" the unknown and unseen driver asked.

"Be just like those three monkeys, partner."

"You got it." He paused. "Good luck. I'm goin' to pull out now. I'll just act like I'm havin' a hard time gettin' clear. Be backin' up and so forth. I'll back my rig right up to the bumper of that raggedy-assed Peterbilt by the car. I'll stay there for a ten count. Time for you to roll under the trailer and do whatever in the hell you're going to do. And I sure don't want to know what it is. Okay?"

Barry grinned.

The driver dropped his rig into gear and began slowly backing up, Barry staying even with the rear wheels, walking slowly, the knife held by his leg.

After several tries, the driver put his trailer bumper just about one inch from the front bumper of the Peterbilt. Barry stepped to the Peterbilt, darted past the tractor and slipped up between tractor and trailer.

He saw the man and woman the driver had mentioned. They were standing near the front of the backed-up rig, looking at it. One of the guards he'd first spotted was looking toward the area where Barry's rig was parked. The other guard had his back to Barry. Barry didn't know what he was looking at.

Whatever it was, it was his last look at anything on this earth.

Barry sprang off the tractor, landed on silent feet, and jerked the man's head back, slicing his throat.

Blood flooded Barry's gloved hand as the man jerked and trembled. Barry lowered the body to the blacktop and quickly fanned the body. A silenced .22 pistol. He checked it. One in the chamber. He clicked the weapon off safety and looked into the right-hand mirror of the truck: the driver was staring at him. Barry lifted the pistol. The driver grinned and revved his engine. The sound was enormous in the night.

Barry lifted the silenced pistol and shot the man sitting in the car with Cutter. The little slug slapped through the rolled-up glass and struck the man in the head. He pitched forward and to one side. The sound of the truck's engine covered the slight noise.

Cutter bailed out of the car, a sack in one hand. She reached back into the car and came up with a club in her right hand. She stood up, took aim, and threw the club with every ounce of strength she had.

The club struck the woman in the head and knocked her completely off her feet just as Barry pulled the trigger three times, aiming at the man with her. He joined his companion on the asphalt.

The one remaining guard disappeared into the maze of 18-wheelers.

Barry quickly piled the immediately accessible dead and wounded into the car and said to Cutter, "Go! I'll catch up with you."

Cutter ran across the asphalt, pausing just long enough to give the woman a vicious kick to the head.

Barry dumped her in the trunk of the car, slammed the lid shut, and pulled out. One side of the woman's head was caved in.

The friendly driver had pulled out and was gone, trucking eastward.

There was a CB in the big automobile and when Barry had Cutter in sight, he blinked his lights three times and flipped the CB channel selector to 3.

"Come on," Cutter's voice reached him.

"Where's the nearest place where some of your people might be?"

"SAC base in Blytheville, Arkansas."

"Too far. Watch for a place where I can set this car in some timber!"

"Ten-four!"

Cutter spotted a place and Barry jumped the shoulder and drove the sedan into timber, floorboarding the pedal, working his way deeper into brush, the rear end howling and fish-tailing.

But it would be, with luck, midday before the car would be found.

Barry waited until a string of cars had passed and then ran from the timber, climbing up into the cab. Cutter pulled out. Barry noticed there was a bruise on her face and her lips were swollen.

"They slapped you around some."

"The woman did. She also mentioned some other rather perverted acts she said she had in store for me. After I got through servicing the entire Islamic Army."

"You won't have to worry about her. Last time I looked, her brains were hanging out of her nose and ears."

"Couldn't do anything except improve her looks. Ugly bitch." She held out a crushed and ratty-looking sack.

"What the hell is that?"

She smiled. "The sandwiches. You said you were hungry, dear."

21

"You got everybody looking for you, Dog," Jackson told him.

West Memphis, Arkansas. At a truck stop.

"The more the merrier. I sure don't want to deprive anybody of their turn at me and Cutter."

"You're in the wringer now, Dog. From here to the coast, you're going to be running the gauntlet. I-7 is looking for you. The Islamic Army is looking for you. The Red Brigade has people gunning for you. The Bader-Meinhof gang has terrorists out in the field for you and Cutter. It seemed that everybody wants a piece of the Dog."

"Bring me up to date, Jackson. How is that guy with the busted ankle?"

"His foot had to be amputated. Crushed too badly to be saved."

"What a shame!"

"I can just tell that you're overcome with emotion."

"The two terrorists that Barnett's people recovered?"

"They're alive. When they've been interrogated fully, we'll probably try to swap them for some hostages in the Mid-East."

"The guy from the motel in Knoxville?"

"Let's say he's still alive." Jackson's answer was given flatly.

Barry got the message.

"There might be some left alive in that car I drove into the bushes," Barry suggested.

"The Tennessee Highway Patrol just found that car about two hours ago. The woman is alive, but she's brain-dead."

"I suppose that American taxpayers are picking up the tab for her hospitalization?"

"Of course."

"So we keep on trucking?" Barry said.

"That's it."

"See you, Jackson."

"Good luck, Dog."

When Barry had climbed back into the truck and settled down behind the wheel, Cutter asked, "Well?"

"The terrorist community has pulled out all the stops, Cutter. Everybody wants a piece of the action. They're all gunning for us."

"What else is new. So? And? . . ."

"We're going to take the goddamnest route to California in the history of trucking."

"Bait, right?"

"Lethal bait, Cutter. Did you check the weather?"

"That early winter storm has blown out of the west; it all moved east. It's cold but clear."

Barry grinned and dropped the big rig into gear. "They tell me that Nebraska is lovely this time of year. Nice and flat and just right for a shoot-out."

"So what are we waiting for?"

They pointed the nose of the Kenworth north, heading into the cold country, straight up Interstate 55. And before they had gone fifty miles, Barry's eyes picked up a tail.

"Pickup truck behind us. Blue Chevy. Man and a woman. I think they're going to try the friendly approach now. Everything else has failed."

"This will, too," Cutter told him.

"I forgot to ask: how'd those goons take you last night?"

"Right in the middle of the truck stop, with fifty drivers

around us. After I got the thermos filled—which we forgot, by the way—the man and woman flanked me. She had a fragmentation grenade in her jacket pocket. Held the pocket open so I could see it. Asked me if I'd like to see a lot of truck drivers die. I learned several years ago, Barry: these people mean it. They're not afraid to die. Not at all. I figured I could stall them long enough for you to get worried and come looking."

"You know, Cutter, unless people like George and several of his colleagues come out openly and support a no-holds-barred type of war against terrorism, this country is just liable to lose this damn conflict."

"That's our consensus, too. So far we've taken a defensive posture. It won't work. We've got to take the offensive and do it so aggressively, people of that ilk will be afraid to screw around with us."

"Hey there, big truck!" the CB squawked.

Barry smiled and reached for the mike. "Which big truck are you talking to?"

"Northbound, just passing the Osceola exit. That's a fine looking rig you've got."

"Thanks. You drivin' that blue pickup?"

"That's a big ten-four, good buddy."

Barry grunted. To Cutter: "Whatever books Comrade X supplied them on CB chatter were a bit outdated."

"I heard that."

"Where you heading, good buddy?"

Another trucker snickered over his CB, but otherwise kept his mouth shut.

"Up into Illinois. You?"

"Oh, me and the wife are retired. We're just seeing the country."

"In a pig's ass," Barry muttered. "But let's play the game." To the CB'ers: "Well, you just sit back there in the rocking chair and relax. We'll take you with us."

"Thanks! They call me the Old Farmer and my wife's handle is Popcorn 'cause she likes popped corn. You?"

"Oh, Lord!" Cutter groaned at the handles.

Barry smiled. "I'm called Loup. My old lady is Poopsie."

Cutter's mouth dropped open. "Poopsie!"

"We'll just tag along behind you and maybe when you stop, we can get acquainted and have some coffee."

"Ten-four."

"Kissy-kissy, good buddy!" an unknown trucker snickered into his mike.

Barry ignored it.

"Poopsie!" Cutter muttered, shaking her head.

"Keep your eyes open for the second team," Barry said, laughing at the expression on her face. "I don't know how long those two behind us are prepared to keep up this charade . . . Poopsie."

Cutter told him what he could do with the handle he'd hung on her. If implemented, a very painful suggestion.

The pickup stayed behind them as they rolled on through the northeast corner of Arkansas and into the boot heel of Missouri. Old Farmer talked occasionally on the CB, and both Barry and Cutter picked up immediately on the absence of 'good buddy' from his chatter.

"Realized his mistake," Barry said.

"I can't spot any second team," Cutter again adjusted the smaller mirror on the chrome mounts.

"I have a hunch they're going to keep the other teams back until they know our destination for sure. We've got a lot of daylight left. There's a truck stop up here on fifty-seven. We'll pull in, get us a thermos and meet Old Farmer and Popcorn."

The man and woman appeared to be exactly what they claimed to be: retired folks. Both of them were in their mid-fifties. Extremely healthy mid-fifties.

They had coffee and chatted for a few minutes, then were back on the road. Neither Barry nor Cutter had revealed their final destination, even though Farmer had asked them twice.

To ask again would have really tipped their hand. But Barry had said they would cross the river at Moline.

"What's your opinion, Cutter?"

She was behind the wheel.

"When I went to the restroom, I slipped out for a fast visual of their truck. I couldn't see any long-range radio equipment, but I'd make a guess that CB is jacked up high. The camper shell is custom built: wood and metal. It'd take an axe to break that door in the back."

"I couldn't pick up any accent from either of them."

"Nor could I. And I've been trained in that field. Their English is just too perfect. Right out of the textbook."

"That's the way I see it. They learned it by rote."

"Nationality?"

"Hard to say. I'll guess and say Central Europe. I'll also guess and say they've been deep cover, sleeping in this country for a long time. Ten years; maybe longer."

"I couldn't pick up any suspicious bulges."

"Nor could I. If they're carrying, they've got them stuck in their boots."

"All right. Let's see what they do when we pull over up here at the weight-watchers."

The pickup rolled on by the co-op and disappeared from sight. When Cutter pulled back onto the slab, the pickup was waiting for them, idling on the shoulder.

Barry crawled back into the sleeper. "Stay on fifty-seven until you get to Salem. Then cut west and pick up fifty-one; that's a two lane. Stay on that to Bloomington. If I'm not awake by then, give me a shout."

"That's a big ten-four, Loopie."

Barry laughed and lay down on the bunk. He was asleep within two minutes.

He crawled out of the bunk just south of Decatur and before he spoke, he checked the mirror. The pickup was still with them.

"How goddamn obvious can a tail get?" he pondered.

"I haven't picked up any sign of a second team. Surely they're not thinking of trying us alone?"

As if magically intercepting their conversation, the CB speaker rattled: "Sure hope you folks don't mind us tagging along. Me and the Missus don't have anyplace to go to in a hurry. Like we told you, we sold our place and bought us a trailer down in Florida. And to tell you a truth: we really admire and respect truck drivers. Kinda makes us feel important to be able to tag along with you. We do this all the time."

Barry picked up the CB mike. Dusk was very gently settling over the land. "That's all right, Farmer. Glad to have the company." To Cutter: "You tired?"

She shook her head. "Not a bit. Bored is the word."

"We'll pick up seventy-four at Bloomington. Take that up to Moline and then eighty all the way across the state. Pull over up there, Cutter." He pointed. "You lie down for a time. No goddamn pickup is going to take this rig alone. First sign of anything out of the ordinary, I'll yell."

Nothing happened. Except that Cutter was asleep five minutes after her head hit the pillow. The pickup stayed with them through Bloomington, took the loop with them around Peoria, and cut straight north with them at Galesburg. At Moline, Barry pulled over for food and fuel.

Cutter had been asleep for several hours, and appeared fresh and rested.

And Farmer and Popcorn also appeared fresh and alert.

Barry wondered about that. Both of them were years older than he was, yet neither appeared in the least tired. Cutter stayed with the truck while Barry went in to eat.

Then he noticed the hands of Old Farmer. Not the hands of a man pushing sixty. As he ate, Barry observed the hands of the woman. Young hands. He again shifted his eyes to Farmer. Fresh cologne. The man was fresh-shaven. Curious. Why would a man traveling, with no particular destination in mind, and no appointments to keep, go to the trouble of shaving several times a day, using an electric razor, bouncing along in a pickup truck?

Sure. A person can dye their hair, use lots of makeup to appear older; but you can't dye whiskers.

"Well, folks," Barry said with a smile. "I guess this is where we part company."

Farmer jerked his head up, a startled look in his eyes. The woman also appeared suddenly nervous. "I . . . well, assumed you were going on west, Loup."

"Well, you see, we haul for the government, Farmer. We really can't tell you where we're going. You can tag along until we get to Iowa City, if you like, but after that, it'd be best if you peeled off and went your way." He stood up. "It's been nice traveling with you two. Hope you have a nice trip. See you."

Barry tossed money on the table, picked up the fresh thermos and sack of sandwiches he'd ordered for Cutter, and walked swiftly to the truck, climbing in on the passenger side.

"Roll, Cutter. There isn't much between here and Iowa City, and that's where they'll hit us. Let's go."

22

"Cute," Cutter said, after Barry explained. "I didn't pick it up. You sure you wouldn't like to come to work for us? We do hire civilians."

"You're just after my body." Barry did his best to act coy.

She laughed. "There is truth in that." She sobered, munching on a ham and egg sandwich. She had shifted up, gained speed, and was on the loop. She glanced in her mirrors. "Time for the second team to make an appearance, don't you think?"

"I've been watching. Nothing yet."

"There's the pickup. That one dim headlight gives it away."

"They won't try anything just yet, I'm thinking. It'll be between Davenport and Iowa City. There are some long stretches there."

They rode in silence for several miles. Barry's Uzi lay on the floorboards, two clips clipped together for faster work. His Beretta was full, resting in the leather of his shoulder holster. Cutter's jacket was open, her .380 worn on the left side, butt-forward. The big .44 mag was tucked down between the armrest and her side.

Barry reached back and pulled a small bag to him. Unzipping it, he reached in and took out several grenades, laying them on the shallow dashboard.

When Cutter swung the rig westbound, on Interstate 80, Barry reached for the mike.

"Go to three, Farmer." Barry switched over.

"On three, big buddy. What's up?"

"Come and get us, motherfucker." Barry switched back to 19. "Get over in the left lane, Cutter."

She swung the rig over.

The pickup began closing fast.

"Here they come," Cutter said.

A bullet pinged ineffectually off the trailer, the howl of the ricochet just audible over the roar.

Cutter jerked her gloved thumb backward. "From them," she said. "I saw the flash."

"Guess that lights the candles and blows them out, huh, Cutter?"

"I guess it does, Dog."

"Cut off all lights."

She plunged the rig into darkness.

"Count five and swing into the right lane."

After a five count, she swung over.

About five seconds later, both felt the pickup impacting with the trailer. The night was torn with the howling of metal against concrete as the rig dragged the pickup along at 65 mph.

"Shake it loose, Cutter!"

She swerved over onto the shoulder, back and forth, from slab to shoulder, until the pickup, what was left of it, was slung free. It went crashing over the side, a shower of mangled metal and glass and blood.

She cut the lights back on.

"Two down," Cutter said tersely. "And maybe a couple more who might have been hiding under that camper top."

"I thought about that, too. Screw em."

"My sentiments exactly."

"Now where's the second team?"

"I think they just pulled in behind us," Barry said, looking at his mirror.

"Can you make out what it is?"

Barry smiled. "I think they're finally getting smart, Cutter. A pair of matched Kenworths."

"Do I kick in the afterburners and blow dust in their faces?"

"Naw. Let's go to war," he said calmly.

"Dog." The voice popped out of his speaker. "You know what channel to go to."

Barry clicked over to 3. "Come on, asshole!"

"No way out of this box, Killer-Dog. Now you die!"

"What group are you?" Barry radioed. "Camel-humpers? Bugger-Badhof? Or don't beat me no more, Boss?"

"Racist honky."

"Racist honky?" Cutter said with a laugh. "Talk about a contradiction in terms."

"Well, I found out who the second team is, anyway. The American version of the Islamic Army. Let's see if I can make him mad." He keyed the mike. "Hey, Leroy! You still there?"

"Swine! My name is Abboud. I tell you this only because you should know the man who is going to kill you."

Barry keyed the mike. "Hey, Abu-Kubooboo! Are you going to fight or bore me to death with words?"

One rogue truck behind them suddenly surged forward.

"Stay in the left lane, Cutter." He picked one grenade up from the dash, pulled the pin, counted and then tossed the lethal pineapple out the window.

Luck was with them that night. The grenade blew just as the truck passed over it. For just one instant, there was a flash and then headlighted darkness. Then the tractor seemed to tilt upward and lurch to one side. Flames began boiling out from under the rig as the fuel caught fire but did not explode. The rig righted itself for a moment, and then went out of control, spinning and jackknifing off the highway, rolling out into the darkness.

"Bye, crap-face." Barry radioed to the others.

"Up ahead, Barry." Cutter brought his eyes from the mirror and the rapidly vanishing pile of twisted metal that was once a truck and trailer.

"Where the hell did those bob trucks come from?"

"Right off that ramp." She nodded her head as they passed the darkened on-ramp.

The bob trucks were running side by side, blocking both westbound lanes of the super slab.

Nothing happened until a ten-or-twelve-truck convoy passed them eastbound. When the slab was clear of any immediate traffic, Barry's CB speaker crackled.

"Your interference has been troublesome, Man-called-Dog. But you may now number your life span in moments."

"Which faction do you represent?" Barry radioed, staying on channel 3.

"Spare me your racist mumblings. We are all brothers in our fight for justice and freedom and equality."

Barry laughed and Cutter smiled. Same old communist dogma. He radioed, "You wouldn't know real justice or equality if it was shoved up your butt, Ahmed."

"You are a crude and despicable person, Dog. Now go meet your maker!"

The doors to the bob trucks were flung open; the headlights revealing a half dozen men, all armed with automatic weapons, and all pointed at the Kenworth.

"Die!" the voice screamed over the speaker

But Barry had definite views about dying. He had already grabbed up his Uzi and was leaning out of the window, bracing himself as best he could, and hauling back the trigger, letting the Uzi spit and snarl its death song in the night.

He worked the Uzi left to right, fast-changed the clip, and poured another thirty rounds into the now blood-splattered interiors of the bob trucks.

One terrorist slipped and Barry and Cutter watched as his mouth opened in a scream they could see but not hear. He dropped his AK-47 and flailed his arms, trying to maintain his balance on the blood-slippery floor of the moving truck. He fell down and tumbled out onto the slab.

He was mashed into a greasy spot on the super slab, under

the tires of the rig, Cutter making no effort to avoid squashing him like the vermin he was.

Barry had changed clips, placed the Uzi on the floorboards, and had jerked out Cutter's big .44 mag. He put three shots where he felt the driver's head should be, the killer-bullets knocking great holes in the wall. The bob truck slewed to one side and collided with the bob truck in the right lane, knocking it onto the shoulder. The right-lane truck recovered and fell back just as the bob truck in the passing lane left the slab and went rolling out into the grassy median, turning over end over end.

Barry reloaded with the speed-loader just as Cutter, without being told, roared up alongside the remaining bob truck. Barry emptied the .44 mag into the cab of the truck and then Cutter was past them, putting the pedal to the metal. The big Kenworth, with its custom-built engine, screamed westward, howling like an enraged wolf.

The driverless bob truck left the slab and went sailing to the right, tires spinning and biting into emptiness. It landed on all wheels and broke apart, bodies being flung into the cold night air.

Barry reloaded the .44 mag and laid it on the dash, jerking up the mike. "Come on, Camel-breath!" he challenged. "Let's mix it up some more."

But the truck behind them had slowed and was exiting south on highway 6. They wanted no more from Cutter and the Dog.

Not on this night.

"Another time, Dog," was the parting message coming out of the speaker.

Cutter took the mike. "We'll damn sure be waiting for you, buddy-boy."

"Despicable woman! You will die hard, bitch!"

Cutter's face tightened and she began tracing his ancestry back across the sands—or perhaps, the south side of Chicago. By the time she got through, they were out of normal CB range.

When Barry finished laughing, he said, "Did anybody ever tell you you're pretty when you're angry?"

But Cutter was in no mood for jokes. She pointed a gloved finger at the CB speaker. "Buttholes like that give me a royal pain!"

"You'll get no argument from me about that, Cutter." He was punching fresh loads into empty clips for the Uzi.

Cutter was barreling westward on the super slab, about twenty miles east of Iowa City. She checked the speedometer and slowed down to sixty. She took several deep breaths and calmed herself. "And they hate women," she added.

Barry kept punching live loads into clips and offered no comment.

Cutter glanced at him and a slow smile curved her lips. "Sorry. I do get carried away at times."

"I understand."

"Do you, Barry?"

"Yes. I think so. I think I know what you're saying. Just like my dad, I worked very hard, eighteen and twenty hours a day for years to build my business. Dad would have sent me through college, but I chose to work my way through. Education is available for anyone who wants it. If not formally, they can educate themselves. No one has the right to remain ignorant and expect something for nothing. Am I close?"

"Yes. But what is disturbing to those of us who have dedicated our lives to stamping out terrorism, is this: many, if not most terrorists are really quite intelligent."

"In book sense," Barry countered. "They lack common sense." He smiled.

Cutter caught the smile. "What's so funny?"

"We've just killed a dozen men and women. And we're riding along having a philosophical discussion, without either of us showing any signs of remorse. Have we become as callous as the people we're fighting?"

"In a way. That's just part of the hazards involved in this job. To successfully combat terrorism, one has to understand it, and when one does, one faces going off the deep end."

Barry laid the recently filled clips for the Uzi in the small bag. He took the grenades off the dash and placed them in the bag and zipped it closed. He holstered the big .44 mag and stowed away the freshly filled speed-loaders.

"All tidied up," he said. "All in a day's work, I suppose is one way of looking at it."

She glanced at him. "Regrets, Barry?"

"About tonight?"

"About what we're doing?"

"Not a one. Way I look at it is this: the cops, the badge-carrying men and women, are just barely holding their own. To tell you the truth, I'm really beginning to think there might be some loss. So somebody has to be out here, hip deep in crap, trying to balance the odds. That's me. And for a time, you."

"Something else my people told me back in Knoxville, Barry."

He waited.

"My new orders have already been cut. I'm heading for Europe."

"When we get to California?" Barry guessed.

"Yes."

She smiled.

He looked at her. "What are you smiling about? Are you that damn anxious to get rid of me?"

She laughed at him. "No. But it's like I told the guys back at the motel."

Again, he waited.

"I told them it might take us quite a while to make this run."

He smiled at her. "Next rest area we come to, pull in."

"Why?"

"I'll show you when we get there."

"Is it vegetable, animal, or mineral?" She grinned.

"Pure animal."

23

Cutter was still sleeping when dawn broke forth behind the westward-bound rig.

Both knew that this joining together would probably be the last, and Barry made it last as long as he could physically hold back.

Now they were a few miles east of Des Moines and the weather had turned colder.

But a car had been following the rig for many miles, and Barry suspected conditions were about to warm up considerably.

"Cutter!" he called over his shoulder. "Get your pants on, kid. I think we're about to have company."

She dressed quickly and slid up front, her eyes checking the mirror.

"That black car behind us?"

"That's the one. And I'm thinking something else, too: we're causing them too much grief. Costing them too many lives and bringing too much attention to them. No matter how much they'd love to have the cargo they think we're carrying, I believe we've taken top priority."

"And they'll use whatever is at their disposal to take us out." Statement.

"That's the way I see it."

"Have you played cat and mouse with them yet?"

"Not yet. I thought I'd let you get a few more minutes of sleep."

"So let us get on with it, boy." She lifted the carpet and tugged open the compartment, taking out one of the sawed-off pump shotguns. The shotguns were loaded with three-inch magnums, pushing number 2 buckshot.

She ka-shucked a round into the chamber.

Barry slowed down. The car behind them slowed. He speeded up. The car behind them speeded up.

Barry glanced at a map, and at the next junction, headed northeast on 65. "There isn't a town for about forty miles, Cutter. First good turnaround, let's get out of this rig and take the fight to them, how about it?"

"Suits me fine. I need to stretch my legs anyway."

"You want a shotgun?"

"Naw. I'll stick with the Uzi." He glanced at his mirror. "Well, well, now! We have more company joining the parade."

Cutter glanced into the left-side junior west-coast mirror. "I'd say so. Can you make out how many are in that lead car?"

"Four, I think. Four to a car makes twelve, Cutter. Hell, that's just six apiece. We got them outnumbered."

They rolled on for another ten miles, and that put them smack-dab in the middle of nowhere.

"That looks like a real good place right over there, Barry." She pointed to an abandoned farm complex.

Barry turned in and drove right through the chained and locked gate with the sign: ABSOLUTELY NO TRESPASSING BY ORDER OF SHERIFF'S DEPARTMENT.

The Kenworth smashed the gate flat.

The three cars followed, but had fallen back, unsure of what the Dog was doing.

"We going to step out and just start shooting, Barry?"

"Sure are," he said cheerfully.

"We don't even know they're terrorists."

Barry had stopped. The three cars had stopped. Barry noticed CB antennas on the trunks of all three. He picked up his mike.

"Get ready to bail out." He stuffed a grenade in each jacket pocket and then lifted the mike to his lips. "This is the Dog. Come and get me, assholes!"

Both of them jumped from the truck as the cars surged forward, rear tires kicking up gravel as they spun forward.

Cutter jerked the shotgun to her shoulder and punched a hole in the windshield and tore off the face of the driver of the lead car. The car went out of control for a few seconds until the man on the passenger side could grab the wheel and step on the brakes.

Barry leveled the Uzi and held the trigger back, completely ruining the day for the men in the second car. He was changing clips when Cutter's shotgun roared three times, as fast as she could pump it.

He heard the sound of bullets hit her body and out of the corner of his eyes, watched her fall.

He took the fight to the terrorists—those who remained. And they were trying to get out of the car.

Barry pulled the pin on a grenade and rolled it under the car, then dove for cover, pulling Cutter under the trailer as he went.

The car went up like a small atom bomb, and Barry figured they had the trunk filled with explosives. He rolled Cutter over and checked her. Shoulder and side wounds; but they were clean, the slugs passing through and then exiting out. There was not a large amount of blood flowing, just a small ooze.

The debris had stopped falling and all that could be heard were a few moans.

Barry muscled Cutter into the cab of the Kenworth and got the hell out of there. One terrorist, with more guts than sense, stepped in front of the Kenworth, waving a pistol.

Barry ran over him.

"Say hello to Allah, crap-head!"

* * *

Barry got back onto 65 and headed for Des Moines. He reached for his CB mike. Cutter's voice stopped him.

"No," she said, her voice surprisingly strong. "I have ID that will keep me out of trouble. Gunshot wounds have to be reported to the police, you know. Besides, you don't know the rules we operate under. The mission comes first, Dog. So you just drop me off in Des Moines. I can take care of myself."

Barry opened his mouth to protest, then closed it, knowing she was right.

"How's the pain?"

"Not bad. Yet."

He knew what she was saying. He'd been there himself more than once.

With a grimace, she reached behind her and pulled out a small bag, taking out a first aid kit and plugging the wounds temporarily. She took a clean jacket from another bag and shrugged out of her bloody jacket.

"What's the drill, Cutter?"

"First truck stop we come to, you pull in, I get out, and you get the hell gone."

There was nothing more to say.

24

She had kissed him quickly, with pain in her eyes, and had climbed out of the cab. She had walked into the truck stop without looking back.

She had told Barry not to interfere, not to make any phone calls on her behalf.

Just go!

He went.

But there was pain in him, too. Not the physical kind. That heals. The kind that stays with a person for a long, long time.

He hit the loop, picked up 80, then 35, and once more pointed the nose of the truck west. He clicked on the radio, searching for news.

There was plenty of news, and not all of it good.

The news commentator was bemoaning the discovery of several more bodies of known world terrorists, including two that the Israeli Mossad had been after for years. The bodies had been found alongside Interstate 80 in Iowa during the early morning hours.

Barry clicked off the radio before the guy could really get wound up.

He wondered how Cutter was doing.

Then, like a big dog, the Dog shook himself and pushed the lovely Cutter out of his mind.

He knew one thing for sure: he was operating on adrenaline and needed some rest in the worst way. He checked his maps and at a truck stop, called an AFB just inside Nebraska and told them he was coming in.

Two hours later he was waved through the gates of the base and a security vehicle led him to a closed compound. Wearily, he crawled out of the rig and was met by Captain Barnett and his team.

"How's Cutter?" were the first words out of his mouth.

"She's going to make it. But it was close. She'll be transferred to an Air Force hospital as soon as possible. You look beat, Barry. Come on. Jackson's on his way in. Seems you've really turned the heat up under the butts of the terrorists and we want to keep it hot. But right now, let's get you fed and bedded down for a few hours."

When he opened his eyes, Barry was slightly disoriented. He lay for a time in the warm and comfortable bed, getting his thoughts all together.

He checked his watch on the nightstand. Almost five o'clock. Damn! he had slept for nearly twelve hours. He couldn't remember the last time he'd done that.

Throwing back the covers, he padded to the john and took another shower, standing under the hot needle spray for a long time. He dried off and dressed warmly, for the weather had turned cold and nasty.

The base was beginning to stir, coming to life. Barry stepped out into the hall of the BOQ and nearly ran into an Air Force security man, startling them both.

Barry smiled at the young man. "Am I under guard?"

"Oh, no, sir! I was sent to wake you up at six. You're due at a meeting at oh-seven hundred hours."

"Right now, I'd like some breakfast, if you don't mind."

"Not at all, sir. Just follow me."

They stepped outside and the foulness of the weather really smacked them both in the face. Bits of freezing rain mixed with snow filled the dark morning air.

Barry had lost all track of time. He wasn't even certain what month it was. He asked the young security guard.

"Fifteenth day of December, sir. Christmas will be on us before we know it. You going home for Christmas?"

Barry smiled, a smile mixed with sadness. Home? What home? he thought. I'm dead and buried in New Orleans. My home is that Kenworth parked out there, armor plated and with enough weapons stored inside to start a minor war. Home? No, young man. I'm not going home.

"No," Barry forced a smile. "I'll probably miss going home this time."

"That's too bad, sir. I start leave on the twentieth. Going back to Ville Platte."

Barry smiled and spoke to him in fast Cajun French.

The young man laughed and replied in Cajun. "I thought I heard some bayou in you, sir."

Then they were at the officers' mess and the young man was gone.

"Au revoir and bonne chance," Barry muttered to the back of the Cajun boy, up in the land of snow and ice. "Light one of the bayou bonfires for me."

He stepped inside the warm mess and Barnett waved to him.

Barry returned the wave and fixed a tray of food, walking over to the table where the special operations team was sitting.

"Sleep well, Barry?" Sergeant Halleck asked.

"Like that much talked about rock. I don't think I moved more than twice in twelve hours." He looked at Barnett. "News of Cutter?"

"She's fine. To quote the doctor, 'She's strong as a horse.' "

Barry remembered the punch on the arm she'd given him. The bruise had only just recently begun to fade. "Good. So bring me up to date about this meeting I'm supposed to attend."

The special ops team was seated well away from anyone else. Barnett sipped his coffee and said, "Certain people in government, both here and abroad, say thanks for that operation yesterday, Dog."

"My pleasure."

"The Mossad, the French DST and SDEC, along with British SDS, SAS and SIS and certain units in Germany like your style. Also a couple of units in Spain. You're welcome in those countries anytime you'd like to go. Just thought you'd like to know what you're doing is appreciated by some."

Barry smiled. "Be kind of difficult to take my rig to France, wouldn't it?"

"Speaking of your rig, it's been serviced and restocked. You'll be back on the road by noon today."

"I'm ready."

"Going to lone-wolf it?"

"Yes."

"Plans?"

"I'm going to drive that rig right up to the front door of that so-called mosque in California and then drive it right through the place."

"That's going to upset the man called Ja," Barnett said with a chuckle. "Besides, how do you know where the mosque is?"

"Cutter told me. She okayed it with Jackson," he added.

"Yes," Barnett said softly. "I know. You're really going to do it, aren't you?"

Barry nodded.

"Going to go up against thirty of forty or maybe a hundred armed people, alone!"

Barry shrugged philosophically. "I'm told I'm expendable."

Lieutenant Jamison said, "We have intelligence that says certain terrorist factions are preparing to move against the families of Stanton and O'Neal."

"I was expecting that. I don't have to tell any of you that terrorists are just like any night-riding bunch that ever lived. They're cowards." Barry shrugged again. "It's like I've always said: best way to turn a hanky-twisting liberal into a gun-totin' right-winger is to have some violence touch a member of his family. If any harm comes to just one kin of George Stanton, you best turn the volume down on your TV, 'cause George's liberal days are over."

Barnett nodded his head in agreement, but there was a look of sorrow on his face.

Barry picked up on it. "What's the matter?"

"There aren't enough available agents to protect everybody we need to protect, Barry. You know that. We can't cover his aunts and uncles and cousins. The Bureau and Treasury and, hell, everybody is stretched thin as it is."

"We tried to warn George and Bonnie. I tried, Cutter tried."

Barnett buttered a piece of toast and spread jam over that. He munched for a moment. "I hate you tell you this, Barry. But," he sighed, "the terrorist groups have put a contract out on your dog."

Barry's face hardened so quickly it startled even the combat-hardened Barnett. "Anybody hurts Dog, I guarantee you, it will take them three very long days to die. And like certain Indian tribes use to say: 'They will not die well.' "

Sergeant Gale said, "I think anyone who would deliberately hurt a pet—whether it be a canary or a dog—is a low-down, no-good, sorry son of a bitch."

The others around the table nodded their heads in agreement. Barnett filled his cup from the carafe and smiled sadly as he stirred in sugar. "I had a little dog when I was a kid. Name was Stinky. Just a mutt. He wandered up when I was about seven, and he was mine and I was his until the summer of my tenth birthday. He was a good dog. But we had a neighbor who didn't like dogs. Real mean bastard. Liked to poison dogs and cats. He was a real lowlife. I went off to visit my aunt and uncle that summer before I was ten in the fall. My momma wrote me a letter; I hadn't been gone a week. Old Man Glascow had killed Stinky. Stinky was walking across the man's backyard and he just stepped out with a club and hit my dog on the head. Hit him so hard it crushed Stinky's skull. Said that was one more goddamn dog he wouldn't have to put up with."

Barnett sipped his coffee. "Stinky never had done the man's yard any damage. Never dug up any flowers or anything like that. I think Stinky was even afraid to crap in the old bastard's yard. I say old. Glascow was about the same age as my dad. Maybe forty. But he was sorry. That October was my tenth birthday. I got me a new bike and all sorts of stuff. But I also got me a brand-new twenty-dollar bill from my granddad. Two dollars for every year of my life. I had found what I wanted out of a sportsman's catalog, but didn't have the money to buy it—until then.

"It was one of those survival type slingshots. Steel frame and with enough power to kill somebody at long range. Providing you could hit them. I waited for a damn month for that thing to come in. It was a beauty. And I'd had enough money to order me some spare rubber for it. And all that month I'd been scrounging around gathering up ball bearings and just the right-sized rocks and buying a bag of marbles here, two bags there, so on. I must have ridden my bike all over half of Dallas gathering up materials."

He sipped his coffee and smiled in satisfied remembrance. "It was good winter time I got started with my plan. I'd buried Stinky right on the edge of our property, way in the backyard, right where that son of a bitch had to see it every time he looked out his kitchen window. And it pissed him off, too. He told my dad it did. My dad told Glascow if he didn't like to look at it, he could damn well move.

"My dad liked Stinky too." Barnett chuckled. But there was precious little humor in it.

"I made life miserable for that son of a bitch. From my upstairs bedroom window, I got so good I could knock out every friggin' window in the back of his house. I busted his car windows. All of them, at one time or the other.

"Of course, he knew it was me. He told the cops it was me. But the cops measured the distance between our houses and told him there was no way I could sling a rock two hundred feet. And nobody knew about my slingshot. No one.

"I put sugar in the gas tank of his car, sugar in his power mower. Ruined both engines. I understood terrorism at an early age, boys. I invented it in my neighborhood.

"It went on all winter. All spring. All summer. I'd skip two/three weeks, he'd slack up in his vigilance, and then I'd let him have it again. Cops talked to me so many times I became an expert in interrogation at age ten and a half. But they never could catch me.

"I cost him some money. Dad said his insurance rates went up sky-high. He had to finally put shutters on all his back windows, floodlights in his back yard—and then I'd promptly shoot them out. I even improved on the slingshot and when I was eighteen, long after Glascow moved away, I had it patented; still get a nice monthly check on that.

"I got brassy about it. I'd call out to him from our property, asking if I could have some of the broken lumber from his window frames so's I could keep a fresh cross on Stinky's grave.

"Took me thirteen months, but I made that son of a bitch move. On the day he moved, he stood on his property, in his backyard, and cussed me and my dad. After he'd gone, my dad said to me, 'I worry about you, boy. Your mind works in a strange way'."

Barnett waved his hand at the other members of the special ops team. "All of them can tell you similar stories, Barry, and you probably have one to tell yourself. I think we understood terrorism at a very early age. Takes a special kind of mind to deal with it."

"Yeah," Barry agreed. "You're right. Did you ever see this Glascow fellow again?"

Barnett shook his head. "Naw. I don't even know where he moved off to. Somewhere in Dallas, but I don't know where."

"Anybody that would hurt an innocent pet deserves whatever comes at him in the night," Sergeant Gale said. "And I might tell you that story sometime. Over a few beers."

Captain Barnett grinned. "See what I mean, Barry? They all have their stories."

"What would you do if this Glascow came through that front door right now?" Barry asked Barnett.

"After all these years?"

Barry nodded.

"Walk up to him, hold out my hand, and then when he took it, break his fuckin' arm."

25

Most of the men in the conference room wore unfriendly looks on their faces. And Barry had the feeling this run was about to end.

Jackson waved Barry to a chair around the long table and got right down to business. "This will be your last run for a while, Barry. There has been a very abrupt change of plans, necessitated by the number of unexplained bodies recently found along our nation's highways."

"Disgraceful!" a man said.

Jackson winked at Barry and Barry began to relax; politics was being played out.

A pinch-faced man with a mouth like a fish looked at Barry. "If news of your involvement with the present administration ever leaked out, the press would have a field day."

"Most shocking news I've received since Watergate," another three-piece suit said.

Barry listened to about five minutes more of the same rhetoric, then all the men got up and trooped out.

When the door had closed, Barry looked at Jackson. "What the hell was all that about?"

"Just a bunch of politicians playing the old game of CYA." Cover Your Ass.

"They've made their views known, so now if I'm uncovered, they're clear."

"That's it."

"What a bunch of crap!"

"That's the way the Washington game is played, Barry."

"Let's get down to the real business."

Jackson wrote two names on a slip of paper and pushed the paper toward Barry.

Ja and Bakhitar.

"I gather they're becoming a real nuisance."

"So I'm told."

"Take them out?"

"With extreme prejudice."

Barry smiled. "Since one is black and the other is an Iranian, that could be construed as a very racist remark."

"When it comes to terrorism, I am totally color-blind." Jackson laid a large manila envelope on the table, put on his coat and hat, and walked out.

Barry looked at the large color blowups. The mangled bodies of men, women and children who had been caught up in a terrorist bombing. Ja was written on the top on that photo. The hideously tortured bodies of a man and two women filled another photo. Bakhitar was the name of that one. There were several more large photographs, all guaranteed to leave the viewer with a sour stomach.

Barry put the examples of terrorism back into the envelope, closed the hasp, and walked out into the cold air.

He spat on the ground a couple of times to get the bad taste out of his mouth, then stood for a moment, breathing deeply of the winter air. Someone had brought his rig around to the side of the building. He walked over to it and climbed up into the cab. All his clothing had been freshly laundered and pressed. The cabin had been spotlessly cleaned. He looked at his logbook and trip tickets. Everything was in order and up to date.

Everything from his room at the BOQ had been packed up, secured in the sleeper.

"What a quaint way of telling me to have a good trip," he muttered.

He picked up his thermos. Filled with steaming coffee. A bag of sandwiches lay on the seat.

Barry dropped the Kenworth into gear and pulled out.

It was snowing.

"Merry Christmas to all," he muttered. "And for Ja and Bakhitar, get ready for a long good night."

He headed south on 73/75 and then turned west on highway 2. Fifty miles later, he rolled onto the super slab. The weather had warmed, the snow turning to rain. The slapping of his windshield wipers kept him company as he rolled on westward.

Cutter came into his thoughts. He rudely pushed her away.

Bonnie entered his mind. He told the little blonde to get lost.

But he silently cautioned her to be careful. The nuts and the flakes and the slime were after her, her family.

The highway called to him, the tires humming on the concrete, the big steering wheel under his hands, the rig responding smoothly.

Several times his CB speaker crackled with friendly voices, calling to the midnight-blue Kenworth, barreling westward.

He did not respond to the friendly calls.

He rolled on at a steady 65 mph. The Dog.

Kate slipped into his mind.

He pushed her away.

A one-man army. Carte blanche in dealing with terrorists. No rules. No Geneva Convention. Offering no quarter, expecting none. A lone soldier in a big 18-wheeler.

A wild, reckless, caution-to-the-wind feeling surged through him. He had nobody. No one at all. He was alone. And would be until the day his luck ran out and he stopped the bullet with his name on it. But he would not go into that long sleep easily. He would go out snarling and growling and biting.

He switched his CB to channel 3. By now it was common

knowledge among the groups he sought that the Dog monitored channel 3.

He lifted the mike to his lips. "This is the Dog. Any of you assholes out there listening?"

Silence.

"I'll find you," Barry spoke to the loneliness of the cab. "I'll find you. And I'll destroy you."

When he pulled into a truck stop at North Platte, his eyes had been watching the station wagon that had been following him for more than fifty miles. His eyes continued to watch as the station wagon pulled in and drove over to the gas pumps.

Two men. Dark complexion, dark hair, mustaches. Solid-built men. Hard-looking.

The electronics boys at the AFB had worked frantically on the rig while Barry slept, installing a warning system that would sound an alarm if anyone tried to open a door, crawl under the rig, tamper with the hood, or just leaned up against any part of the 18-wheeler. Barry didn't really understand how it worked, only that he knew it did.

He flipped the switch and quickly got out of the cab. He had only thirty seconds to do so. He could deactivate the system by punching out a series of numbers on the cigarette-pack-size metal box he slipped into his jacket pocket.

The little box was practically indestructible, so he had been told. The system cost a lot of money, too—so he had been told.

"Wars are usually expensive," had been Barry's reply.

He walked across the parking lot, the empty thermos in his hand, and entered the warmth of the cafe. He would fuel up later; the oversized tanks enabled him to make much longer runs than any standard rig.

He wasn't hungry, having eaten a couple of the sandwiches the mess had fixed for him. He had just wanted to see what that station wagon would do.

He chose a spot at the counter where he could keep an eye on his rig. The station wagon, filled up with gas, pulled around to the four-wheeler parking area and stayed put, the men remaining inside, the motor running.

He lingered over his apple pie and coffee, listening to the chatter of drivers, but taking no part in any of the conversations.

He watched the men in the station wagon and concluded they were pros. They were not in the least impatient. They just quietly waited.

Barry checked his watch. Several more hours until night. But the day was overcast and gloomy, creating a dusklike appearance.

He concluded that the men in the station wagon were going to try to take him out when he left the truck stop, and then probably kill themselves. These nuts believed that was a quick way to enter heaven.

Fine. If they wanted to exit this vale of tears, Barry would damn sure help them on their journey. Just be delighted to do so.

He paid for his pie and coffee and went to the restroom, then slipped out the back way. The silenced .22 auto-loader was nestled in his shoulder holster, ready to spit and snarl its lethal little loads.

He walked to the edge of the building and waved until he got the attention of the two men in the station wagon.

Then Barry gave them the finger.

He could tell they were getting angry; but still they sat in the wagon.

Barry turned his ass to them and walked swiftly out into the truck parking area. Behind him, he heard the sounds of car doors clunking shut.

He slipped under a trailer and knelt behind the rear right side tires, the silenced auto-loader in his hand. His lips were peeled back in a silent snarl. The Dog waited.

He heard one call out. In a language he could not understand but believed it to be Arabic. The other one replied in a stage whisper. Same language. At least it sounded the same.

"Speak English," the one to his right called.

"He didn't go to his truck. He's hiding among these other trucks."

"At least we know the bitch-dog was hurt. That is one less we have to deal with."

"Pity. I would have liked to mount her like a dog. It would have been amusing to listen to her screams."

"No more talk. Go around this truck here. We have him trapped."

Barry smiled and shifted positions silently. The terrorist with pussy on the mind came into view. Barry shot him twice in the chest as rain began to fall. He slipped out as the rain began coming down harder and dragged the terrorist under the trailer and left him. He duckwalked the length of the trailer and once more crouched behind the rear wheels.

The one remaining terrorist was calling for his partner. His calls fell on dead ears.

Barry came out from under the trailer and shot the terrorist twice in the back as the rain began coming down in torrents. The terrorist stumbled and twisted on his way down. He lifted his pistol and Barry shot him again, in the face, the little hollow-nosed bullet going in one eye, and coming out above his ear on the other side of his head.

Barry punched out the right combination of numbers and deactivated the alarm.

Working very quickly, Barry put both terrorists in his trailer and resealed the doors. They'd both be gamey by the time he reached the coast, but with any kind of luck, maybe he'd have more bodies to deliver to Ja and Bakhitar by then.

In the big custom sleeper, he stripped, dried off, and changed into warm clothing. He dried off his little .22 auto-loader and loaded the clip up full. Back under the wheel, he pulled slowly out of the parking area and rolled back onto the super slab, heading for Wyoming.

He turned on the radio and tuned into a country station, turning the volume up on a song by Dolly and Linda and Emmy Lou.

By the time the station wagon was reported to the cops and they ran the license plates, Barry would be well into the next state, and no one back at the truck stop would have any special reason to remember him.

Barry smiled.

All in all, he thought, it had been a very productive afternoon.

26

The rain changed to snow about fifty miles from the Wyoming border. Big, fat, wet flakes that were already sticking due to the rapidly falling temperature. By the time he'd rolled into the outskirts of Cheyenne, the roads were becoming icy and Barry said to hell with it and pulled over to get him a room at the first nice motel he found.

He could have traveled north a few miles and nighted at an AFB, but he thought to hell with that. He had all this super electronic warning gear, so let it work while he rested.

He patted the back of the trailer on his way to check into the motel. "Nighty night, boys. Don't let the bedbugs bite."

Sometime during the night the storm blew out of the state and went roaring on eastward. But just to be on the safe side, as far as the weather went, Barry pointed the nose of the Kenworth south on Interstate 25, and stayed on it.

It was still slow going until he got south of Denver, and there, he began to make a little time. He spent the night in a motel in New Mexico and had not spotted any tails all day.

As it so happens this early in the season, the next day turned out to be shirtsleeve weather as Barry headed south, picking up Interstate 40 west at Albuquerque.

Those two in the back were really going to be ripe if Barry didn't do something and do it quick.

At a truck stop, he bought some tarps and some heavy tape

and spent a few disgusting and very odious minutes wrapping the two and sealing them shut.

They were just as ugly in death as they had been in life.

He spent the next night in Las Vegas, pulling out hours before dawn and rolling hard. At noon, he was on a two-lane, just north of Bakersfield, heading for Interstate 5. He was about seventy-five miles from the headquarters of the so-called religious leader named Ja.

Ja was, in truth, about as religious as Attila the Hun and about as faithful to his god as Hitler was to preserving the human race.

There was absolutely, positively nothing on the stretch of highway Barry was traveling. Ja had chosen well if he wanted solitude . . . and a place to train his Liberation Army of Islam.

Barry drove past the entrance to Ja's headquarters twice, just to let them know he was in the area—he knew hidden guards would spot the rig—and then barreled north on a secondary road, finally cutting back east and checking into a motel many miles north of Ja's HQ.

He took a hot shower and dressed for dinner, knowing that it could very well be his last time to put on a suit—until the undertaker stuffed cotton up his butt and brushed his hair and knotted his tie before placing him in his silk-lined home for eternity.

Barry slept well that night, dreamless, and awakened refreshed. He ordered breakfast sent to his room and ate slowly, savoring every bite. Then he geared up: the 9mm went into a shoulder holster, the .44 mag on the other side. His jacket covered them, but he couldn't zip it up.

Outside, Barry squatted down on the concrete walkway and looked at his rig, mulling over some things in his mind. Then he smiled.

He punched off the alarm system, paid his bill, and pulled out. Several miles down the road, he pulled over and transferred the bodies from the trailer to the cab. He wired them with explosives, almost gagging at the stench, and then taped the tarp closed.

But he left the windows down.

Bastards smelled awful!

Back in the trailer, he opened all the compartments and wired the explosives to activate from an electronic timer. He put that in his pocket. He patted each stiff and tarped terrorist and rolled on.

"Lovely day, isn't it?" he asked one mummy-look-alike.

No reply.

"That's all right," Barry told him. "Just relax and enjoy the ride."

It was a short one. Before he knew it, he was approaching the locked and chained gates to the headquarters of Ja. He floorboarded the pedal and blew his air horn and barreled right on through, as the two guards leaped for safety.

It was the weirdest-looking building he had ever seen. Purple stars and silver moons and blood-red suns all adorned the multicolored House of Islam that Ja built. Having constructed the hideousness on the blood of innocents around the world, Barry thought it only fitting to bring it down with some blood of its followers.

Cutting a wide donut in the middle of the barren front of the mosque, he leaned over and opened the right-hand door, shoving the tarp-wrapped terrorists out. They bounced on the sunbaked ground and rolled to a halt.

All sorts of gowned and robed and turbaned weirdos were running out of the huge headquarters of Ja . . . and bless their little religious hearts, they all had guns of nearly every make and model and caliber.

All pointed at Barry's rig.

The lead started whining and bouncing and howling off the armor plate and thick bulletproof glass of the Kenworth as Barry continued in his wide circle in the front of the HQ.

Several of the terrorists made the deadly mistake of getting in front of the rig. They moistened the parched earth for a while with their blood, the big tires mashing them flat under the midmorning sun.

As a dozen or more gowned and turbaned figures ran toward the rolled-up bodies of the terrorists, clawing at the tarp, Barry felt that was just a dandy time to go exploring at the back of the funny-looking sprawl of buildings. For when they removed the last bit of tape and peeled back the tarps, things were going to get really hostile around there.

Barry made it to the rear of the mosque when the explosives, almost simultaneous in their eruptions, ripped the air. He had wired enough explosions around the bodies to stop a tank.

A huge dust cloud arose from the front of the building, the dust all mixed up with the twisted guts and mangled limbs of a dozen or more terrorists who had gone to pay their last respects to their fallen comrades in terror.

Barry circled the complex and the last thing several members of the Army of Islam saw, coming out of the whirling dust, was the massive front of the Kenworth, its huge steel-protected grill bearing down on them, a death-grin on the face of the man called the Dog.

Their anguished screaming was cut off in burbling chokes as the tires ended careers in spreading death worldwide.

As Barry slowed to make another circle of the complex, terrorists jumped onto the rig, hanging on the chromed ladder, beating at the thick glass with fists and the butts of pistols.

Barry headed for a wooden building at the edge of the complex, picking up speed as he went, and silently praying to whatever god—if any—looks after men like him, that the building was not filled with explosives, Barry crashed into the wooden structure and barreled out the other side. He completely destroyed the small shack, and doing that, ripped off the turban-toters who had been clinging to the sides of the rig.

Glancing into the mangled and glass-busted right-side mirror, Barry saw one terrorist impaled on a sharp board, the board ramming clear through the man and pinning him to the earth. His legs were still kicking in anguish, seconds before death would reach down with that cold hand and touch him.

Barry made one more circle, the roaring of the mighty engine and the kicked-up dust adding more confusion to an already chaotic scene. He saw four people run to a car parked away from the complex, and recognized one as Ja. He spun the wheel, felt the rig try to roll, and brought it under control, heading for the car.

"Not yet, ol' hoss," Barry muttered. "Just stay hooked for a little while longer."

He rammed the side of the car, turning it over, the impact almost tearing his gloved hands loose from the big steering wheel.

He drove the car into the side of the mosque, smashing it, maiming or killing those inside. Barry dropped the shift into reverse, backed up, and felt the big engine shudder as he floorboarded the pedal, lunging forward, again making a wide donut in the front of the complex.

He widened his donut, giving the rig all the power he felt it could take, and at the final turn, unlocked the fifth-wheel slide. He heard the connections rip as metal tore loose and the trailer ripped free, to go rolling over and over, smashing into the entranceway of the HQ, completely destroying the front wall.

Barry pointed the nose of the Kenworth toward the west, toward the dirt road that would lead him back to the highway, and as he did, he flipped the detonator switch on the little box in his shirt pocket.

Just as his tires touched concrete, the headquarters of Ja, the squashed leader of the now-defunct Army of Islam, went up in a roar of several hundred pounds of plastic explosives.

The ground shook even at that distance, Barry feeling the mighty charge transmitted through the tires, up through the suspension system to the steering wheel and through the leather of his driving gloves.

Barry drove to the interstate, waited until no vehicles were in sight, then grabbed his suitcase and shrugged out of his twin shoulder holsters, leaving them in the cab of the truck.

"Sorry," he muttered. "Jesus, I hate to do this."

He tossed a thermal grenade with a delayed timer into the cab and closed the door. He began walking up the interstate, catching a ride on his fifth try.

"Down on your luck?" the elderly man asked, smiling at Barry.

"No, sir." Barry said brightly. "All things taken into consideration, I guess I'd have to say that my luck has been pretty darned good."

27

He had caught a bus at a one-store-stop just off the interstate, changed a couple of times, and made it to Vanderberg
AFB in the middle of the night. At a stop, he had called Jackson and told him to advise Barnett that he was coming in.

Barnett met him at the front gate and promptly took him to
a motel in Lompoc.

"Man, man, you're hotter than that much talked about two-
dollar whore, Barry. Have you heard any news at all since you
blew up Ja's HQ?"

"No, none. What's it sound like?"

Barnett chuckled. "God, that must have been quite a show
you put on. Something like seventy bodies have been found
and the cops think they'll probably find at least ten more once
they get through digging through the rubble. Of course none
of the cops can say it out loud—hell, they have to be careful
who they even think it around—but they're pleased that this
terrorist group is out of business. And, brother, you damn sure
put them out of business."

"Ja has been confirmed dead?"

"Squashed like an ugly bug. But Bakhitar and a lot of his
bunch were not at the mosque. And neither was Darin Grady
or any of his people."

"I need a new rig."

"One is being readied for you now. It'll take about a week,

with people working around the clock, to get it ready. You'll pick it up outside of Marysville one week from today."

"How's Cutter?"

"She's been transferred to an Air Force hospital. She's fine. Up and walking." He looked at Barry and smiled. "And your dog, Dog, is all right."

"What am I to do until my rig is ready?"

"Lay low. Tomorrow we'll get you out of this motel and move you to L.A. Sleep. Eat. Relax."

"Is my rig going to be identical?"

"Yes. But with a lot of new features and modifications. You'll enjoy them all."

For a full seven days, Barry did nothing but eat and sleep and read and watch TV, especially the news programs. Many of the networks' news men and women were shocked by this rash of violence sweeping America, several of them imploring the government to do something about it.

Barry got a big hearty belly laugh out of that.

If the news people would ever decide which hand washed the other, the government would be more than happy to do something about crime and terrorism. Delighted, in fact.

"Make up your mind, people," Barry muttered, rising to cut off the TV. He stopped abruptly as the anchorman's expression turned hound-dog somber.

"It is with great regret and heartfelt sorrow that we report the death of George and Edna Stanton, the parents of our own George Stanton. Mr. and Mrs. Stanton were killed when their car was struck by a truck and forced off the road near Allentown, Pennsylvania late this afternoon. The truck was found abandoned several miles from the scene of the accident and a large manhunt is now under way for the driver . . ."

The picture faded and a commercial about something that was guaranteed to make you shit came on the screen.

Barry clicked off the set and fixed himself a drink, sitting back down. "Accident, my butt!" he muttered. He picked up the phone and dialed Jackson.

It was answered on the second ring.

"You heard?" he asked Jackson.

"About ten minutes after it happened."

"I hope you're not going to tell me it was an accident."

"I was born looking like I was retarded. That doesn't mean I am. Hell, no, it was no accident. The Pennsylvania State Police know it was no accident, so does the local sheriff's department and everyone else involved. But they were asked to play it like it was. For obvious reasons."

"When do I come out of retirement?"

"You grow that beard like Barnett asked you?"

"Sure did. Looks halfway decent now."

"What color is it?"

"Salt and pepper. More salt than pepper. And I got a professional dye job yesterday. I look like I'm about due for retirement any moment."

"The word had gone out via our leak—yeah, we found him and we're going to use the bastard for a while—that a shipment of grenades and rocket launchers is leaving Southern California in two days, en route to a small military reservation in Vermont. And yes, there is one there."

"I never doubted you, Jackson."

"You'll pull out day after tomorrow. Your rig is ready for your inspection. A car will pick you up in about two hours. I was just going to call you. I wanted to see how the network was going to treat this thing about George's parents."

"Screw the networks. Who'll be coming after me this run?"

"Everybody," Jackson said cheerfully. "Good luck." He hung up.

"You didn't have this rig built in any week," Barry told Barnett.

"No, we didn't. The U.S. Treasury seized it about two years

ago in a drug-running operation. A certain government agency has been working on it for about that long. This baby will stop damn near anything anybody wants to toss at it. The glass is the finest made anywhere. It'll stop a fifty-caliber machine gun slug. The tractor was flame red when it was seized. How do you like this color?"

Barry liked it, but it had taken a few minutes for it to register on him. Midnight black with white striping. The colors of a Husky. He smiled. "I like it."

"Look inside."

Barry climbed in. Real leather. And damn expensive leather at that. Soft.

Barnett had climbed in the other side. "I'd like to tell you that it has machine guns and rocket launchers built in the fenders and under the hood, but that's not feasible. But it was suggested. But it will give you an honest one hundred and twenty miles an hour. With this radio"—he pointed—"if you're within a hundred miles of any sort of military base, you can talk to anywhere in the United States. If you don't want to use the radio, there is a mobile phone." Again he pointed. "The sleeper is custom made. Big bed. A special built bed for Dog . . ."

Barry looked and laughed. Damn sure was!

". . . Small refrigerator, small john, TV and radio, plenty of storage space." He pointed to the floor of the sleeper. "In there, anything and everything you might need in the way of weapons, plastic, grenades, ammo—you name it, and it's in there. You are a legitimate SST, Barry, with all the papers to prove it. If you are stopped by the police, you won't be detained long. And we'll know where you are at all times. S.O.P. for all SSTs. You'll be tracked, every move, from a bunker at the Energy Department's Safeguards and Security Division command center at Kirtland AFB, Albuquerque. Ninety percent of the cops will be cooperative if they stop you. The other ten percent are local hotdogs and we've dealt with those types before. Take whatever action you think is necessary to get your job done. You've got thirty-six hours to familiarize yourself with this rig. Have fun."

He pulled out two hours before dawn, an average-built, gray-haired man with a salt-and-pepper beard driving a beautiful midnight black custom Kenworth; a truck that carried more armor plate and bulletproof glass than any other rig running the super slab. A rig that held, in secret compartments, an Uzi, two sawed-off shotguns, a 9mm Beretta, a silenced .22-caliber auto-loader, a .44 magnum, a 7mm magnum sniper rifle, and five thousand rounds of ammunition. He carried an assortment of grenades and plastic explosives, with various types of timers and detonators. Under the floor of the trailer were various other types of heavier weapons and ammunition, weapons which Barry could not imagine himself using, much less getting to in a tight spot, but if the government wanted to load him down with machine guns and bazookas, that was fine with him.

By the time the sun poked its growing warmth and radiance over the eastern horizon, Barry was halfway to Las Vegas. A rolling target for terrorists.

He missed the company of Dog and knew that dog missed the road, for the animal loved to travel.

Barry wondered when the terrorists would strike at him, and how. Barnett had echoed what Jackson had told him: "Everybody will be coming after you, Barry. The ante on your head has gone up to a quarter of a million dollars. Stay loose, Dog."

On the seat beside him lay a small M-11, the lethal little machine gun not much bigger than a large auto-loader pistol. It fired a .380 round (9mm Kurz), and while the smaller .380 does not have the knock-down power of its larger cousin, the 9mm, the .380, when fired from the M-11, has a nasty habit of chewing the hell out of its intended target. The weapon was fitted with a sound suppressor, not only to reduce the noise, but to help stabilize the weapon on full auto; firing without the suppressor, the muzzle would climb very rapidly.

A bag of 32-round clips lay beside the little spitter.

Barry wore his .22 auto-loader, with factory silencer fitted, in a shoulder rig, under his jacket.

Five hours after leaving Los Angeles, Barry rolled past Las Vegas. Due to the carnage he'd already caused on some of the nation's highways, those responsible for his routing put him on a wandering route; for the most part, avoiding those states whose cops were already a tad jumpy from all the bodies that had littered their roadways.

His route, as it now stood, subject to change, was L.A. to Vegas, Vegas to Salt Lake City. Then up into Idaho, where he would then cut east, rolling through Wyoming, South Dakota, and into Minnesota, down to Chicago, over to Cleveland, up to Buffalo, and then into New England.

No one actually believed he would ever get to Vermont; the attack, or attacks, would come long before then.

And all available intelligence stated that Darin Grady would lead the attack against him.

Barry wondered if the Irish terrorist had new front teeth by now.

He rolled on at a steady 65 mph, rarely answering any calls on the CB, and keeping his eyes open for any sign of a tail. But he could spot nothing to arouse any suspicion in him.

Just at dusk, he pulled into a motel south of Salt Lake, and carefully parked his rig, setting all the alarms, much more sophisticated ones than were on his other rig. And he also had, in his suitcase, a small handheld electronic sweeper that would enable him to detect if any explosives had been planted on the outside of his rig. The explosives he carried were in specially constructed compartments, built so as not to confuse the sweeper.

He climbed down to the asphalt and walked around his rig, making a visual check, inspecting the seals and the locks in his trailer doors. The locks themselves were very expensive; they could not be cut or sawed open, even if the alarm system was not working.

The coming of dusk had dropped the temperature sharply, but the weather people had said there was no chance of any snow. Just clear and cold.

Leather scraped on the asphalt behind him and Barry instantly dropped to the parking lot, rolling under his trailer.

"Take the son of a bitch alive." The voice was gruff and accented. "Darin wants him alive for some fun."

28

Barry rolled and came up on the other side of his trailer, swinging his metal suitcase at the head of a dusk-darkened man. The suitcase caught the man on the side of his head and dropped him like a brick. Shifting the suitcase to his left hand, Barry filled his right hand with the silenced .22 auto-loader and put two huffing rounds into a short stocky man who suddenly appeared before him.

Barry was rolling under the trailer even before the man had dropped to the cold asphalt, two slugs in his heart.

Barry was very careful not to touch any part of the trailer, for only a few pounds of pressure would activate the alarms, and the cops were the last thing Barry wanted right now.

He did not know how he sensed it, but he felt there had been three men. And two were down. One was dead or dying, and the second one surely had a busted skull or a very bad concussion.

That left one.

The lights from a car pulling into the motel filled the parking lot. Barry peeked around the tire he crouched behind and looked directly into the startled eyes of a man squatting on the other side of the big tire.

Barry jammed the .22 into the man's face and pulled the trigger three times. The terrorist cried out once, and slumped to the asphalt, his blood staining the blacktop.

Barry cursed softly.

Now he had three bodies, right in the middle of a motel parking lot, and didn't have any idea what car they might have come in, if any.

Barry crouched behind the tire for a moment longer, trying to come up with some plan for disposal of the bodies.

The man he'd bopped on the head with the metal suitcase groaned and moved.

Barry lifted the silenced .22 and pulled the trigger. The man jerked once and was still.

His headache had been cured.

Permanently.

He felt he had no choice in the matter. Reaching into his jacket pocket, he deactivated the rig's alarm system and moved to the rear of the trailer, unlocking the doors.

He wondered why the motel seemed so quiet. And so little traffic coming in and out. Then it came to him.

It was Christmas day.

Moving swiftly and cautiously, he muscled the limp bodies into his trailer and relocked the doors. He leaned against the rig, catching his breath, trying to decide what next to do.

He was parked to the side of the motel, the office on the other side of the building, so it was doubtful anyone had seen him pull in.

A cop car drove slowly up the street, but neither cop even looked his way.

He climbed back into his rig and pulled out. He was tired, over his ten-hour limit behind the wheel, but felt he had no choice in the matter. He began to breathe a little easier when he hit the interstate and the lights of the town faded behind him.

On a deserted stretch of Interstate 15, Barry pulled over on the crest of a long hill, so he could see the lights of any traffic from either direction, and dumped the bodies of the terrorists, rolling them down into a deep ditch.

Working very fast, Barry wet a towel and wiped away the blood stains from the floor of his trailer. He would get rid of the towel up the road a piece. Fifty miles later, he found a nice-looking motel and pulled in and checked in. He showered and dressed and had a martini while waiting for dinner.

Why hadn't he spotted his tail? Where had the terrorists come from?

Unanswered questions.

He was cautious walking back to his room, but nothing lethal came out of the night at him. Double-locking his motel room door, Barry laid the auto-loader on the nightstand beside his bed and dropped off into sleep, and surprisingly, he slept well.

He rolled out at dawn, after having alerted Jackson's people about the events of the past night and where, approximately, he had dumped the bodies.

The voice told him to be careful.

Barry felt the suggestion to be more than a bit redundant.

"Thank you," he said. "I certainly shall."

On the loop around Salt Lake City, he picked up a tail.

A Datsun 280z, a man driving and a woman beside him. As they edged closer, Barry could see the man was wearing a suit or a sport coat and tie. The woman also appeared to be neatly and nicely dressed.

Just a couple out for a spin the day after Christmas.

He watched as the man lifted something to his lips. Barry began working the channel selector on his CB, pausing at channel 11 at the sound of a voice.

". . . sure it's him?"

"One ordinary truck driver does not take out three of our good people. It's the Dog."

All right, fine. He was getting tired of this damn beard, anyway.

"Go on around him and move on ahead. I'll come up."

Barry smiled and lifted his mike. "Why don't you all come on up and let's rock and roll, assholes?"

A few seconds of silence and then a very familiar voice came through the speaker. Darin Grady. "Pig!"

"No, no," Barry corrected. "I'm the Dog. You be the pig."

Darin cursed him while Barry laughed. That old familiar wildness began rearing up within him. This was where he belonged. On the open road. The Dog belonged to no one and no one belonged to him.

The Datsun accelerated and came up fast. The woman looked up at him. She was really quite pretty.

Barry smiled at her.

She smiled back.

He gave her the finger, then picked up his mike. "Which way do you like it, honey? Considering the company you're keeping, you must like it Greek."

The woman twisted in the seat and cursed him, her face turning mottled and ugly with hate.

Barry laughed at her.

A car behind them began tailgating, forcing them to get out of his way. They pulled up, then swung back over into the right lane. There was no point in any charades; everybody knew where the other stood. It was now all out in the open.

In his mirrors, Barry watched as a big fine luxury car moved up behind him and stayed. Two men in the front seat, two men in the back. And he'd make a bet that one of them was Darin Grady.

But one thing Barry was almost certain of: they wouldn't try anything until they got outside of Salt Lake, and probably not until late afternoon, which would put them up in Idaho.

Barry lifted up the mobile phone and the mobile operator came on. He gave her Barnett's mobile phone number. The phone in his car could not be reached. He tried Jackson and got him, bringing him up to date.

"You want to put an end to this crap, Jackson?"

"Name it."

"I'm in Salt Lake City. Probably seven good hours of daylight left. I'm about two hundred miles from Pocatello. I'll be on fifteen from there on into Butte. You suppose Barnett and his boys would like to get in on this?"

"I know they would. Hang tight. I'll be back with you in about five."

Jackson took a little longer than five minutes, but he did get back. The news was not good. "The security lid has clamped down tight, Barry. Some damn oversight committee chairman got wind of the Air Force's special ops team and the Air Force sent them all to bull's ass, Italy, or some damn place, until the heat cools down. But it doesn't, by God, mean I can't get in it."

"Jackson! . . ."

"I'll be on an Air Force jet within the hour. You pick me up at the airport in Pocatello. That's the Municipal Airport."

"Jackson! Damn it, Jackson, listen to me. You're the President's man. You . . ."

But he was talking into a dead connection. Jackson was on his way, taking revenge for the brutal murder of his son uppermost on his mind.

And Barry didn't blame him one damn bit.

Barry played cat and mouse with his tails for a couple of hours, taunting them and cursing them. Then, right in the middle of the Caribou National Forest, they vanished. Barry took that opportunity to pour the coals to his rig, the needle hanging right on ninety and to hell with the highway patrol.

When he was close enough, he called the airport in Pocatello and told them to page a Mr. Jackson and tell him to rent a car and meet his contact at the northbound rest area just south of Blackfoot.

Barry got there and waited; still plenty of daylight left.

He didn't have a long wait. Jackson pulled up and climbed in, tossing a small bag in the sleeper compartment and placing a paper sack on the floorboards. He shook hands with Barry and said, "Where's the company?"

"I lost them just south of Pocatello. You make arrangements for the rental car?"

"Yeah. They're picking it up. Sandwiches and a full thermos of coffee in the bag. Jesus Christ, but it's cold up here."

Barry unwrapped a thick sandwich and poured a cup of coffee. He jerked his thumb toward the sleeper. "Take that Uzi back yonder. While I was sitting here I hooked some clips together for you." He looked at Jackson's heavy outer gear. "Looks like you're familiar with this part of the nation, though."

"Oh, back in my younger days I helped chase some goddamn felons all over this part of the state. A little bit east of here, over around Grays Lake."

"You catch them?"

"I killed them," Jackson said flatly. "They'd shot and killed a federal game warden. Goddamn poachers. I hate poachers." He took a big bite out of a sandwich and both men chewed and sipped coffee in silence until their appetites had been appeased.

"Dog," the low voice came out of the CB.

"Darin Grady," Barry said, picking up the CB mike. "What do you want, prick? You're interrupting a late lunch, or an early supper, one of the two."

"Where are you, Dog? Or are you afraid to tell me?"

Barry laughed in the mike. "Afraid? Afraid of a baby killer like you? You have to be joking."

Darin cursed him. There was a slight slurring to his words, as if he was speaking through an empty space in his teeth.

Barry pulled out onto the super slab before he answered the terrorist. "You want another taste of my boot in your mouth?"

Wild screaming cursing.

Jackson shook his head in disbelief.

Barry keyed the mike. "I'm on the interstate, potatohead. With the lights of Blackfoot in sight. Do you have enough sense to read a map and figure that out?"

"Tonight, you die, Dog!" A new voice was added. This voice was mush-mouthed.

"That's Bakhita," Jackson said. "I have his voiceprint on file."

"Got your cute little turban on, Bakhitar?" Barry radioed.

The Chicago-born so-called religious leader cursed him.

"One on one, Darin," Barry challenged him. "Just you and me. How about it?"

Silence. For a moment, Barry thought the man was going to pick up the glove. Then Darin's chuckle came thought the speaker. "No way, Dog. I loathe and despite you, but I am not a fool. I will admit that I doubt that I could take you. One on one. But we will take you this night. You and your revenge-fevered Treasury man. Good afternoon, Mr. Jackson."

Jackson cursed, loud and long. "That means we've got another leak. Damn it all to hell!"

Barry handed Jackson the mike. "Yeah, I'm here, you son of a bitch!"

"Make your peace with God, Treasury man. For tonight you will see your son in hell!"

Barry turned on all his lights and flickered them twice. He leaned on his air horn and let out a wild Rebel yell that nearly caused Jackson to mess his underwear.

Barry took the mike and shouted, "Come on, Darin and Bakhitar and all the rest of you malcontents. I've been squashing you bastards like bugs all over this nation, and I'll do the same to you tonight. So come on if you've got the balls to do it!"

With a roar of laughter, Barry leaned on his horns.

Jackson reached behind him and picked up the Uzi, chambering a round.

Barry reached down into a bag and laid several grenades on the dash and then unzipped his jacket and wedged the big .44 mag under his right leg.

Several vehicles were coming up fast behind them.

"You ready to rock and roll, Jackson?"

"I've been ready, Dog. So let us get it on."

29

"It makes no sense," Jackson said. "They're coming at us with cars. It would take a tank to stop this rig."

"They've got something else in mind," Barry agreed. "Maybe to knock out the tires with some sort of rocket. I've been expecting something like that for several weeks."

"But if they do that while we're rolling, there might be a wreck, and they couldn't get their hands on the cargo."

Barry thought back. "They've tried to stop me numerous times; it never worked." He shook his head. "No. I don't think it's the cargo anymore, Jackson. I think it's me."

"I think you're right. So we get ready for anything, right?"

"You got it, Jackson." He swung over into the passing lane. "You get the first shot, pal. So get ready."

Jackson's face held a worried look. Barry studied it for a second and picked up on the concern.

"I know, Jackson. All they've done so far is talk, right? They haven't fired a shot or made even one hostile move, right?"

"Stupid of me to feel that way, isn't it, Dog?"

"No," Barry said flatly and firmly. "It isn't stupid to be a good cop. And ninety-nine percent of the cops are just that: good cops. But don't worry, Jackson—they'll make a move. They always have."

No sooner had the words ceased their echoing around the cab, when a late-model sedan roared around the car containing

Darin, and slipped over into the right lane. The sounds of slugs banging off the right-side passenger window startled Jackson, even though he knew the thick glass would stop a .50-caliber slug. He flinched and cursed.

"Your move, Jackson," Barry said calmly.

The sedan had roared on past the 18-wheeler.

Jackson rolled down his window and the interior was filled with icy night air. Barry picked up speed, staying in the left lane. Jackson leaned out of the window, the Uzi set on full rock and roll, and let it bang.

The slugs from the Uzi pocked and spiderwebbed the rear window of the car, the scene highlighted by the lights from Barry's rig. One man's head seemed to explode under the impact of the hot lead. He was flung forward, his blood reddening the back of the front seat.

Jackson changed clips just as Barry pulled up almost even with the car. The driver glanced up at the 18-wheeler, a startled look on his face. He had been counting on the speed of the car to outdistance the big rig. He now realized he had made a tragic error.

His last one.

Jackson lowered the muzzle of the Uzi and let the machine gun sing some death songs in the cold night, the 9mm slugs turning the interior of the sedan into a rolling, wildly out-of-control funeral parlor. The car went sliding off to the right, flipping over, and disappearing into the darkness.

The car behind the big rig slowed and then pulled over to the shoulder. The Datsun suddenly appeared, exiting off the super slab.

"Looks like they've had enough for the time being." Jackson rolled up the window and popped in a fresh clip.

"They had to be sure we were armor plated and bulletproof. They sure as hell don't mind sacrificing people."

"Get ready for anything from Bakhitar and his nutty bunch," Jackson cautioned. "He's totally bananas."

"They won't do anything for another fifteen minutes or so."

The lights of Idaho Falls shone silver in front of them. A pool of light in the cold darkness. "So let's have another cup of coffee and a sandwich."

Coffee poured and sandwiches unwrapped, Jackson looked at a map. "I think we're going to be in for it after Idaho Falls, Dog."

"Yeah. That's the way I see it, too. About a hundred and twenty-five miles of damn near nothing except interstate. We'll fuel up here. Take turns going to the john."

"You got a cigarette?"

"No. I put them down. I thought you quit a long time ago."

"I just started back."

They were back on the road in half an hour. Jackson had bought a carton of smokes and was puffing away.

"How come you're so nervous, Jackson? You're no cherry when it comes to killing people."

"One thing I forgot to mention, Barry . . . The load you're hauling?"

"Yeah?"

"It isn't fake."

Barry looked at him, disbelief in his eyes. "You mean. . . ?"

"Some deep thinker among the powers-that-be felt it would add authenticity to the run. You're hauling rocket launchers and grenades."

Barry sighed. "That's just dandy, Jackson."

"I just knew you'd be thrilled."

The lights of Idaho Falls faded behind them and the super slab stretched before them. They rolled on in silence for a few miles.

"From this point," Barry said, "we've got about twenty-five miles of nothing. And our friends popped up behind us a few minutes ago." Barry studied his mirrors for a few seconds. "Way back. I don't understand that."

He reached for his CB mike. "What's the matter, boys and girls, lose your nerve?"

No reply.

"Is that vehicle in our lane, or what?" Jackson asked, his eyes staring straight ahead.

Barry looked at the headlights and felt a slight chill form in his stomach. It rolled over and lay sluggish and damp.

"Remember the Marine barracks in Lebanon?" he asked quietly.

Jackson swallowed hard. "Yeah. Suicide attack. A car loaded with explosives."

"That's what we got coming at us, partner."

"Wonderful." Jackson lit another cigarette.

The vehicle drew closer. Barry could tell it was traveling at a very high rate of speed. And that just might work against the terrorists . . . if he could time it right.

If he couldn't . . .

He pushed that out of his mind.

"Can you tell what lane he's in, Jackson?"

"Left lane."

"Yeah?" Barry pulled over into the left lane.

"Have you lost your mind?" Jackson asked.

"I hope not. If I can pull this off, we'll make it. If not, someone is going to have to close this section of Interstate."

"Your words are so comforting."

"Thank you. Hang on."

"My butt is drawn up so tight now I'll probably never crap again."

The headlights were right on top of them when Barry cut the wheel. Because of the height of the 18-wheeler, he knew the driver of the death car would be blind from the headlights that Barry had punched on bright. He muscled the rig and held on as the left side tires wandered off the shoulder and onto the frosty grass as they came out of the curve. For a few gut-wrenching seconds, Barry thought he'd lost the rig, the trailer tires slipping and grabbing for traction on the frost-covered grass.

The driver of the car, blinded from the intense light, left the super slab and sailed off the road. A shattering roar ripped the night and flames shot up a hundred feet or more into the air. The explosion was so heavy both men could feel the concrete beneath them tremble for a second.

They roared on through the night.

"Barry?"

"Yeah, Jackson?"

"You got a john in this rig, don't you?"

"Right back there."

"Good." Jackson disappeared into the large custom sleeper and dropped the leather flap.

They crossed the Continental Divide and dropped down into Montana. Traffic was very light, and those who seemed to be bent on killing him had vanished.

But Barry knew they would be back; they would not give up the hunt.

Barry was beat, operating on pure nerve and adrenaline. He pointed to the mobile phone. "Call the Butte PD, Jackson. Tell them who you are and what we're pulling. Tell them we've got to have some rest and can they guard this rig for a few hours."

It took the Treasury man only a few short minutes to pull a lot of strings.

"They said come on in. The rig can be parked in the impound area and they'll assign officers to blanket it. They're also alerting the state police and they'll assist. We cut east at Butte, don't we?"

"If I can keep my eyes open long enough to get us there."

Barry slept for ten hours, having managed to pull off his boots before falling on the big king-size bed. He took a long,

very hot shower, shaved off his beard, and then ordered breakfast sent to the room. He knocked on Jackson's door—the
rooms were adjoining—and told him to come on in.

"You had breakfast?"

"About two hours ago," the Treasury man said. He held a
cup of coffee in his hand. "I went down to check on the truck.
The cops were curious, but managed not to ask any questions."

"We end it today, Jackson." He looked out through the just
opened drapes. "Or tonight, as the case may be."

"How can you be so sure?"

"Trust me."

"I do. That is what's so scary."

They pulled out at three that afternoon. One Montana highway cop had asked, "Either one of you know anything about
a terrible explosion down in Idaho last night?"

Naturally, neither Jackson nor Barry knew a thing about it.

"Uh-huh," the cop said. He looked at Barry. "You got a
handle?"

Barry met his eyes. "Dog."

Something flickered in the trooper's eyes. A slight smile
came and went very quickly. "I thought it might be. Try to be
a little more tidy driving through Montana, will you, Dog?"

Jackson looked slightly confused. "That guy know you,
Barry?"

"Hell, Jackson. Half the cops in the nation know about me."

"That's frightening, Dog. That so many people are so upset
about crime, they would condone a man like you. And don't
take that the wrong way. You know what I mean."

"The people are frightened, Jackson. And you can't blame
them. Let's go."

The weather, for this time of year, was surprisingly good.
Very clear up in the Big Sky country, and lowdown cold.

Just a tad over two hundred miles from Butte to Billings,

nd another two hundred and fifty miles from Billings to the
Iorth Dakota state line.

And anywhere along the way, Darin and Bakhitar and their
ollowers could be waiting.

Barry hoped they were. This had been an exceptionally long
un—he wasn't sure how many weeks he'd been under the gun,
terally and figuratively speaking. And a smoldering anger had
een building deep within him for several days.

Barry had hated night riders all his life. He felt angered by
he loss of George Stanton's parents. A cruel, vicious act, by
ruel and totally unprincipled men and women. Men and
vomen without one shred of decency in them.

Barry intended to rid the world of a few of those types of
eople this night.

And he had his spot all picked out. Providing the terrorists
vould let him get to it.

He did not realize he was smiling until Jackson mentioned
t.

"I'm ready to take the fight to them, Jackson. I'm ready
or a good old-fashioned ambush. How about you?"

"That's a sneaky little smile you've got, Dog. I'm afraid to
ven ask what's on your mind. But I will. What's up?"

A highway sign told them that Bozeman was twenty miles
way.

"Look on your map, Jackson. Tell me what you see between
Billings and Roundup. On highway eighty-seven."

Jackson looked. "Hell . . . nothing! About fifty miles of
bsolutely nothing." He glanced at Barry and smiled. "Oh, I
ike it, if we can pull it off."

"We'll pull over first chance we get and dig out the heavy
ardware in the back. Can you fire one of those rocket launch-
rs, Jackson?"

"Sure. Nothing to it." Again, he smiled. "I like the way
our mind works, Dog. Providing, that is, we're on the same
ide. I would damn sure hate to be your enemy."

Barry gave up trying to find a rest area, and pulled off onto the shoulder. He handed Jackson a tube and all the rockets he could stagger with and then pulled out an M-60 machine gun from the compartments. He set a case of belted ammo on the shoulder, relocked and sealed the doors, and they were on their way.

"I'm going to guess and say Darin and the others have, just like we do, jacked-up CBs. Do you have any intel on that?"

"All their vehicles we've managed to recover so far have jacked-up CBs. No reason to think they'd change now."

"Okay. Even if they should call for us, we don't answer. I'm going to get up here just off the slab, on eighty-seven and start hollering. I got a plan. If it works, we'll be rid of Darin Grady and some others . . . for good."

Jackson didn't answer. Barry knew he was thinking of his dead son. At least Jackson and family thought they had buried the right son.

It had been sort of hard to tell amid all the shattered pieces of American servicemen.

30

The miles and the hours rolled by. Barry and Jackson said little; they were both thinking of the showdown in the cold just a few miles up ahead.

Barry picked up highway 87 north and drove just to the city limits of Billings. There, he got on his CB, staying with the channel he'd previously heard the terrorists using.

After only a few minutes of slurs and profane insults, he was answered.

"Dog! You've been elusive this night."

"Not anymore, Grady. I'm having to take a different route, punk. I'm on eighty-seven out of Billings. North. Come and get me if you've got the nerve."

The terrorist was immediately suspicious. "What are you trying to pull, Dog?"

"Other than deliver a load, I'm trying to kill you, you bastard!" Barry was honest with him.

"I don't trust you, Cur."

Barry then proceeded to insult Darin's mother, father, brothers and sisters—in a very profane manner. And he was driving north on 87 as he did so.

The terrorist cursed him, as did the heavy voice of Bakhitar, and then the speaker fell silent.

"All we can hope is that they took the bait," Barry said, driving through the freezing cold night.

There was no traffic. None. And Barry hoped it would re main that way.

Midway into the Bull Mountains, Barry pulled the rig ove at an intersection and parked it. The night was very cold, s he left it running and locked the doors.

"Over there," he told Jackson. "I'll be up there." He pointe to an upthrusting of rocks. Jackson turned, carrying his heavy load. Barry's voice stopped him. "No survivors, Jackson. No this time!"

The Treasury man's face was hard in the night. "I didn' intend to take any prisoners, Dog." He turned and vanishec into the darkness, taking up his position.

Settling down among the rocks, attempting the impossible in trying to find a comfortable place, Barry knew that just as soon as Darin found the truck running and the doors locked he would know it was a trap. But Barry was counting on the man's wild hatred for him to push him on, to override common sense.

Car lights appeared in the distance, coming from the south. Barry and Jackson had no walkie-talkies, no way to communicate. Everything now was in the hands of fate, as fickle as she might be.

The car lights just kept on coming. Barry counted eight vehicles. The various terrorist groups were throwing everything at him. The word had gone out: Kill the Dog.

As the lead car, a big luxury car that Barry had first guessed Darin was in, approached the parked and running rig, some warning light must have flashed on in the driver's mind, for he gunned the car and tried to make a run for it.

Jackson fired a rocket and the car exploded in the night, the flames leaping about, casting a wild, surreal light to the night and the surroundings.

Barry opened up with the M-60, pouring a hundred rounds into the last vehicle, a station wagon, and crippling the vehicle, killing the occupants, and blocking the rear escape route south.

Jackson fired another rocket and another car became a pile

of ruined burning rubble, cooking the men and women trapped inside.

With Jackson on one side of the intersection and Barry on the other, the terrorists had no chance. When they leaped from their cars, they were cut down. They had no place to run and no darkness to hide them, for the flames from the burning vehicles turned the night into bloody dancing day. The M-60 became so hot it began to malfunction. Barry picked up his Uzi and raked the battleground.

Then nothing moved before them.

He darted from his cover, running to the blood-soaked, body-littered road. Jackson joined him. If a terrorist was found to be still alive, one shot ended that.

Bakhitar was found alive, on the ground, propped up against the side of a car. He glared at Barry through eyes filled with unreasonable hatred. He was bloody from neck to belly.

"You should have stayed in the Windy City, punk," Barry told him, then shot him between the eyes.

Darin Grady had been thrown from the luxury car when the rocket impacted, igniting the fuel tank. There was not much left of him; but then, there hadn't much to him when he was alive.

The woman and man in the Datsun were still in their seats, shot all to hell.

There were no survivors.

"Now what?" Jackson asked.

"I got a load to deliver," Barry told him.

EPILOGUE

Barry lay on the motel bed, watching the news. Dog lay on the floor by the bed, sound asleep. The new year had come and gone. Jackson was back in Washington. Cutter was out of the hospital and recuperating somewhere in Europe.

For a week, certain civil rights organizations publicly deplored the ambush in the Bull Mountains of Montana.

George Stanton had been fined seventy-five dollars for punching the director of the United States Civil Liberties League on the nose.

George then went on TV and delivered a report on terrorism. The liberal had become a conservative.

Barry's bedside phone rang. Jackson.

"You got a million bucks on your head, Dog. Everybody from Qaddafi to Abu is after your butt."

"It's so nice to be wanted."

"How do you feel?"

"Rested and ready to go."

"Your rig is ready to go. It'll be delivered to the motel in the morning. Orders will be hand-delivered in about ten minutes. Good luck." He hung up.

A knock on the door.

Bonnie O'Neal stood smiling at him. Barry waved her into the room and closed the door.

"Jackson thought it would be nice if I gave you an envelope. Since I was coming down here anyway."

"All right."

She took off her jacket and stared at him.

"The envelope, Bonnie."

"Oh, it's on me . . . somewhere. Since you're such a cautious man, I thought you might want to search me for a weapon or something like that."

Barry smiled at her. "Now that might take all night, Bonnie."

It did.

William W. Johnstone
The *Mountain Man* Series